NO ESCAPE

Balanced on the balls of his feet, Zach awaited Frayne's rush. He had been in knife fights before. But not against someone Frayne's size, wielding a knife that could cleave his skull like an overripe melon. Frayne feinted, and Zach retreated, or tried to. He had nowhere to go. His back was to a wall.

A savage gleam lit Jack Frayne's dark eyes. He flicked the Bowie to the right, then the left. But he was not trying to cut Zach open. Not yet. Frayne was toying with him. "Any last words before I bury this to the hilt?"

Zach skipped right and feinted left and went right, and he was almost in the clear when a big hand closed on his shirt and he was brutally slammed against the wall. He cracked his head, hard, and the alley spun in a macabre dance. The same hand closed on his throat.

"I'm going to enjoy this, breed."

The alley stopped spinning and Zach saw his own Bowie poised for a fatal thrust....

#45
WILDERNESS
IN CRUEL CLUTCHES

David Thompson

LEISURE BOOKS   NEW YORK CITY

Dedicated to Judy, Joshua and Shane.

A LEISURE BOOK®

April 2005

Published by

Dorchester Publishing Co., Inc.
200 Madison Avenue
New York, NY 10016

ISBN 0-8439-5458-2

Printed in the United States of America.

Visit us on the web at www.dorchesterpub.com.

IN CRUEL CLUTCHES

Chapter One

Captain Phillip Dover loved the *Astoria* more than he did his wife. When he stood in the wheelhouse and gazed out over the trim white decks, he got a thrill he seldom felt when he gazed at Martha, who after bearing him five children had become as broad as a paddle wheel.

Dover never let on to his wife how he felt. He would rather face a hurricane on the open sea than Martha's wrath, and she was already mad a lot these days. She complained that he did not spend enough time at home. She complained that he neglected the children. She complained that he did not buy her enough clothes or keep their larder well stocked.

He tried to explain that the life of a steamboat captain was not easy. That he had many important responsibilities to deal with on a daily basis, and he left the details of managing their household to her. As he put it during their last argument, "You are, after all, the woman of the house, and dealing with petty concerns is your job, not mine."

That did not go over too well.

As a result, Captain Dover was spending more time on

David Thompson

his vessel than ever. So it was that he happened to be on the forward deck when two of the best carriages money could buy or rent clattered down Front Street to the dock and stopped. Ordinarily, he did not pay much attention to such things, but when the uniformed driver scrambled down to hastily open the door, his curiosity was piqued.

Out of the first carriage stepped a vision of pure beauty. A woman so incredibly lovely, Captain Dover felt a stirring where he had not felt a stirring in more years than he cared to dwell on.

She was dressed all in black: black shoes, black dress, black gloves, black hat. A natural complement to her raven-black hair. Her face was exquisite, the kind that should be enshrined in a portrait for posterity. Her figure was positively enticing. In fact, Captain Dover decided she was just about as shapely a female as he had ever gazed upon, and he had gazed on a lot.

The vision of loveliness regarded the *Astoria*, then turned and said something to someone in the carriage.

Out climbed a young girl. Captain Dover assumed it must be the woman's daughter. At least, the girl had black hair, and from where he stood he thought they both had green eyes but he could not be sure. There any resemblance ended. The sunny yellow dress the girl wore did not match her mood. She stared at the *Astoria* in great sadness, and when the woman took her by the hand and led her toward the gangplank, she balked and dug in her heels.

That was when two men dressed in dark suits slid from the other carriage and hurried to the woman's side. They had dark complexions and dark hair and more than a trace of Creole blood. They were the same height and the same muscular build and looked enough alike to be brothers. Twins, even. At a word from the woman in black, they each grabbed one of the girl's arms and followed along.

In a rare act Captain Dover greeted them himself, with

2

a courtly bow to the lady and a grin for the girl that was not returned. "Welcome on board, madam. Am I to infer you mean to book passage on my ship?"

"Why else would I be here?" the woman said rather haughtily. Then she fixed her piercing green eyes on him and bestowed a ravishing smile. "My apologies. The past couple of days have been most distressing, and I'm afraid I've become a bit snippy."

"Think nothing of it," Captain Dover said gallantly. He tried another grin on the girl, but she was gazing angrily off into the distance.

"Ignore my niece, Captain," the woman said. "She is in one of her peckish childish moods." The woman graciously extended her gloved hand. "I'm Athena Borke, by the way. These are my servants, Carlos and Mateo. And yes, I would like to book passage for the four of us. That is, if you are bound for New York City as I was told?"

"We leave with the morning tide," Dover assured her. "Permit me to say that you have chosen wisely. The *Astoria* is the newest and most luxurious ship in all of New Orleans, and our accommodations are second to none."

"Which is why I chose you," Athena Borke said. "I never settle for less than the very best. You do have berths available, I presume?"

"Our first-class cabins have all been taken, I'm afraid," Captain Dover informed her. "But our second-class are every bit as elegant as the finest you will find elsewhere."

"Didn't you hear me? Second class will never do. I want four first-class cabins for myself and my servants."

As much as Dover was smitten by her beauty, her imperious air was mildly aggravating. "In that case, you must either book passage on another vessel or wait until the *Astoria* returns."

"There is a third option," Athena said. "You can tell whoever is in two of your finest adjoining cabins that you are sorry, but there has been a mix-up and the cabins are already taken."

The preposterous notion made Dover chuckle. "Honestly, madam. That would be highly unethical."

"What price do you place on your ethics, Captain?"

"I beg your pardon?"

"You understand me well enough. How much to bend your ethics and make an exception in my case? Would a thousand dollars suffice? Per room? Beyond the price of passage, of course."

Captain Dover's smile faded. He studied her and her companions anew and noticed things he had not seen before. Important things. Like the hard glint in the woman's eyes and the icy arrogance of her features. Like the unmistakable stamp of latent cruelty on the faces of Carlos and Mateo. Like the fear buried deep in the eyes of the little girl. "You *really* want those cabins," he stressed.

"I thought I had made that clear." Athena impatiently tapped a flawless shoe. "Yes or no? I am a busy woman and cannot abide being kept waiting."

Dover's mind was racing. Something was wrong here. No one paid that much without good reason. Either she was in a dire hurry to reach New York City, or someone was after her. He looked at the girl again and had a troubling thought. But two thousand dollars was two thousand dollars. "You ask a lot of me. I will inconvenience people and earn their ill will."

"So? For that much money, I should think you would slit your mother's throat and dump her overboard, and good riddance."

In his time, Dover had witnessed vicious fights between mates and roustabouts, seen the *Emerald Queen* blown to high heaven with all her hands and passengers on board, but none of that shocked him half as much as the heartless comment from this stunning beauty. For a fleeting in-

4

stant he saw into the depths of her soul, and he nearly shivered at the revelation. "Very well, madam. I will make the necessary arrangements. You may board in an hour."

"One more thing," Athena Borke said, and glanced toward shore. "Is there any chance the *Astoria* can depart earlier? Say, tonight instead of tomorrow morning? I am willing to pay handsomely for any extra work it causes you."

Dover had it then. She was definitely on the run. "Out of the question, I am sorry to say. Not that I wouldn't if I could, but the schedule has been posted. And some of our provisions will not be brought on board until this evening. Tomorrow morning is the earliest we can manage."

"Oh well. It never hurts to ask." Athena gestured at the girl. "Come along, Evelyn. We will buy you a new outfit for the trip and be back in an hour to board."

For Dover it was a busy hour. The occupants of the cabins did not take it well, even though he reimbursed them the passage fee. One man threatened to sue. Dover appeased him by promising he could book a cabin on the next voyage to New York City at half price.

True to Athena Borke's word, the two carriages came clattering down the street again exactly sixty minutes after they departed. While she strode the decks with the sad little girl, her two servants transferred trunk after trunk from the second carriage onto the *Astoria*.

Dover watched it all from the wheelhouse. He had sent his mate into the city to make discreet inquiries about the mysterious lady in black, but Hanson had yet to return.

Soon after Borke and her charge disappeared below, the mate finally showed up. He was out of breath and bursting with excitement.

"I found out what you needed to know, Captain."

"Did you indeed? It took you long enough." Dover had found that the best way to keep the crew in their place was by constantly reminding them how lowly that place was. "I would almost suspect you of slacking off."

"Not me, sir," Hanson declared. "I did exactly as you wanted. But I had to go to four taverns before anyone recognized the name." He lowered his voice even though no one could possibly hear them. "Remember that trial a while back? Some half-breed named King was accused of killing two brothers?"

"Vaguely," Dover said. He had read a report or two about it in the newspaper, but then the paper was always filled with lurid accounts of sensational crimes. "What about it?"

"The brothers were named Borke. Artemis and Phineas Borke. Athena Borke is their sister."

"You don't say?" But that did not tell Dover why she was so anxious to leave New Orleans. "Anything else?"

"Word has it that she is in some kind of trouble with the law. She wasn't happy that the half-breed got off and tried to have him killed. I can find out more if I go to the police."

"No, that won't be necessary," Captain Dover said. "You did well. Keep your mouth shut and there will be a little extra in your next pay envelope." When he said little, he meant little.

"Thank you, sir."

Left alone, Dover paced the wheelhouse with his hands clasped behind his back. He was tempted to go down and suggest to Athena Borke that in light of the circumstances, four thousand dollars per cabin seemed more fair than one thousand. He could bring a lot of grief down on his head by harboring a fugitive, even one so lovely.

But then Dover thought of Carlos and Mateo, and how coldly Athena Borke had mentioned slitting his mother's throat, and he concluded that two thousand dollars was more than enough, after all.

Five o'clock came and went. Dover was overseeing a delivery of barrels of rum when two men came up the gangplank and asked to see him.

They were a strange combination. One was a young rake with a flowing cloak and a sword at his waist. The other wore buckskins and appeared to be part Indian.

"Our apologies, *monsieur*, for disturbing you." The rake doffed his hat in a gesture of respect. "My name is Alain de Fortier. My friend and I are here on most urgent business."

"What would that be?" Dover did not like how the half-breed's blue eyes bored into him with burning intensity. The pistols and the Bowie knife the man wore and the rifle he carried added to Dover's unease.

"This is Monsieur Zachary King," de Fortier said with a flourish to his friend. "He and I have reason to believe that a person we seek has booked passage on your ship."

Dover knew before he asked what the answer would be. "Does this person have a name?"

"Athena Borke," de Fortier said.

"And what has this woman done to earn the distinction of being hunted down by two young stalwarts such as yourselves?" Dover stalled to gain time to ponder.

It was Zach King who answered. "She kidnapped my sister." His tone hinted at what he would do when he caught the culprit.

Alain de Fortier went on. "We have heard that a member of your crew was asking about Athena Borke earlier today, and we came as quickly as we could to ask if she is on board."

Dover had another decision to make, and he erred on the side of fattening his purse. "I have never heard the name nor seen the woman. I am sorry, gentlemen, but whoever told you this was misinformed."

"Do you mind if we look around?" Zachary King asked.

"I most definitely do," Captain Dover said flatly. "I will

David Thompson

not have my passengers disturbed." To defuse their suspicions, he added, "But I will be more than happy to let you know if the Borke woman books passage on my ship. Where can I send word?"

Alain de Fortier glanced at King, who wheeled without saying a word and headed for the gangplank. "You must excuse my friend," de Fortier suavely apologized. "He lives in the Rocky Mountains and is not accustomed to our civilized amenities."

Captain Dover had to know. "Isn't he the one who was on trial recently for murder?"

"That was him, yes," de Fortier confirmed. "He has killed many men, my friend has." De Fortier gave Dover a meaningful look. "I would not want to be the one who angers him. His sense of justice is far more violent than mine." Replacing his hat, he said, "I bid you adieu."

As soon as the pair were out of sight, Dover descended to the passenger compartments and knocked on the door to 101. One of the Creoles answered, Carlos or Mateo, he could not tell which, and he asked to speak with their mistress.

With a rustle of skirts, Athena Borke appeared. "Is there a problem, Captain? You look as if the *Astoria* has just run aground on a sandbar."

Dover moved a few yards away in case the girl was in the cabin, and gestured for Borke to come closer. "Two gentlemen were just here to see me," he whispered. "Well, one was a gentleman. The other was a half-breed. Need I say more?"

Her perfect face did not betray a hint of emotion. "I understand, and I thank you for your thoughtfulness." She smiled a smile that did not touch her eyes and went back in.

Dover was going to ask for the money she had promised, but he figured he could wait until they were under way.

Then, if she balked, he could sic his roustabouts on her. Whistling to himself, he returned to the wheelhouse and spent the next several hours brushing up on his charts and dealing with a host of minor matters having to do with their departure in the morning. When next he thought to check his gold pocket watch, it was nine o'clock and the sun had set.

Captain Dover stepped from the wheelhouse. He loved the sight of New Orleans at night. So many lights, so much life, so much marvelous gaiety. He breathed deep of the muggy air and turned to go back in, when suddenly a Bowie knife flashed before his eyes and its razor tip was pressed to the base of his throat.

"Not a sound or you die."

Chapter Two

Zachary King knew the steamboat captain was lying the moment Dover claimed Athena Borke was not onboard. He could see it in the man's eyes. But he wisely did not let on he knew. He did not want to spook his quarry and spoil his chances of saving his sister from Borke's clutches.

Zach would not rest until he did. Evelyn had been abducted because of him. Because he had killed Athena Borke's brothers and then been acquitted. In revenge, she had taken Evelyn and was about to embark for New York City and from there to Paris, where Evelyn would be beyond his reach and quite possibly lost to his family forever.

The thought fueled Zach's simmering rage. He had never been much good at controlling his temper, in part due to his temperament, in part due to how most whites and many Indians treated him because of a fluke of birth. He had been born half and half, and in their eyes, that made him somehow inferior. All his life he had to put up with abuse and scorn, and it had honed his temper as a whetstone honed a blade.

Boots pattered the street and Alain de Fortier caught up

with him. "You handled that poorly, *mon ami*. I am not a frontiersman like you, but even I know that the hunter never lets the prey know it is being hunted."

"Borke is on the *Astoria*."

"I agree. But now the captain will tell her and she will flee with your sister as she has done before."

"Not this time." Zach veered into a gap between a grog shop and a cheese shop. "There is only one way on or off the ship, and I will be watching it the whole time."

They were only a block and a half from the dock, and the gangplank was in full view. Alain nodded his approval but said, "The captain may not appreciate what you have in mind. He has many ruffians in his crew, and we are but two. Perhaps I should go for help. Certain acquaintances who are handy with a gun or a blade."

"This one I do myself," Zach said.

"Not even me?" Alain said in surprise. "What have I done that you should cast me aside when we are this close?"

Zach tore his eyes from the gangplank and placed a hand on de Fortier's shoulder. "*Tsaan hainji.*"

"What does that mean?"

"It is the tongue of my mother's people, the Shoshones. It means friend. Good friend. A friend of the heart."

Alain's brow knit and he scratched his chin. "I think I understand. You are saying you do not want me along because you do not want me to come to harm. Is that it?"

"No," Zach bluntly informed him. "I do not want you along because I do not want you held to blame for what I am going to do."

"Which is?" Alain asked, and when Zach did not answer, he said, "What are you contemplating in that wild head of yours? What can you possibly have in mind that is so terrible?" Alain blinked, and recoiled as if he had been punched. "No. Not that. No matter what she has done, she is a woman."

"In the mountains when a she-wolf turns rabid she is shot."

"Here in the city, things are different. They hang men for killing women. It is the most heinous of crimes." Now it was Alain who placed his hand on Zach's shoulder. "Please, my friend. I do not care to attend your public execution. Turn her over to the authorities. Let them deal with it."

Zach folded his arms across his chest. "Since I was old enough to stand, I was taught that a warrior who does not fight his own battles is not much of a warrior. Artemis Borke tried to incite a war between the Shoshones and the Crows. Phineas Borke tried to kill me for killing Artemis. Now their sister has taken my sister. This is my battle. I let you help before because I could not do it on my own. But now I have Athena Borke where she cannot escape, and as soon as it is dark enough, I will do what must be done to protect my loved ones."

Alain protested, but Zach refused to listen. He let his friend argue until Alain was talked out, and by then the sun had gone down. "It will not be long now."

A lot of people had gone on board the *Astoria* and many had left again, but Athena Borke and Evelyn were not among them. Zach yearned for a glimpse of his sister, if only to confirm she was alive and well.

Zach would never forgive himself for the ordeal Evelyn had been through. Athena Borke took her to get at him, to cause him as much misery and sorrow as she could, and it had worked. He could think of nothing but Evelyn. Nothing but saving her and returning her safely to their parents' cabin high in the Rockies.

His parents were not there at the moment. They had been en route from the mountains to Fort Leavenworth for his trial when his father was badly mauled by a black bear in a freak mishap. The last Zach heard, his father was laid up somewhere on the trail and his mother was tending him.

Zach's wife, though, had made it to St. Louis. So had his uncle, Shakespeare McNair, and McNair's Flathead wife, Blue Water Woman. They had traveled over a thousand miles to be at his trial, and how had he repaid them? By running off after Athena Borke without telling them.

Zach had a lot to answer for. But it would be worth facing their anger if he succeeded. Evelyn came before all else. He had not enjoyed a good night's rest since she was taken, and he would not rest until Athena Borke paid for her crime. Not in court, where her wealth could buy her lawyers capable of having the case thrown out or her sentence reduced to a paltry term in prison. No, the only thing that would suit him, the fate she most truly deserved, was to die.

Windows were aglow in many of the homes and businesses. They were also aglow on the *Astoria*, and the gangplank was bathed in the light of a streetlamp.

"You are about ready?" Alain said when Zach straightened.

Zach nodded. He checked that his flintlock pistols were loaded and loosened his Bowie in its beaded sheath, then handed his Hawken rifle to de Fortier. "I would be grateful if you will hold on to this for me."

"And I would be grateful if you would change your mind and let me go with you," Alain said.

"We have been all through that. If I fail, get word to my wife."

"As you wish," Alain said sullenly.

Zach crossed the street to a freight wagon parked on the other side. He had his approach worked out in his head. Moving past the wagon, he vaulted a fence and hugged the shadows until he heard water lap the shore. Wading in as high as his knees, he stalked toward the *Astoria* until he came to a small pier, and a rowboat a fisherman had left tied to it shortly before the sun went down.

Zach pulled himself into the boat, cast off the line, and worked the twin oars. He had handled canoes many times, and the rowboat was not much different. As he cleared the end of the dock, he swung toward the steamboat, careful to hunch forward so no one on deck could get a good look at him. With luck they would mistake him for a fisherman returning late from a day out on the river.

The *Astoria* was not the only steamboat at anchor. Other stern-wheelers and side-wheelers lined the shore for as far as Zach could see. It was said that a steamboat arrived at or left New Orleans every two hours. Goods were brought there from towns and cities inland and loaded on oceangoing craft bound for ports around the world. The boom in commerce accounted for the city's boom in population. It was now the fifth largest in the country, with over one hundred thousand people calling it home.

Far too many for Zach's liking. He could not wait to return to the peace and solitude of the mountains, where a man could ride for weeks without seeing another soul. Cities, to him, were cages in which he was nothing but another face in the teeming crowds, forced to live by the laws and rules of others. He hated it with every fiber of his being. Almost as much as he hated Athena Borke.

The thought of her brought a snarl from his throat. Zach had never wanted to end the life of anyone or anything as much as he wanted to end hers. She and her brothers had caused his family unending heartache. Now one of the people he cared for most in the world was in her cruel clutches. She deserved what he would do to her.

Zach had heard it said that no man had the right to set himself up as judge, jury, and executioner. But if he didn't save Evelyn, who would? His wife, Louisa, and Shakespeare McNair were leagues to the west in Kansas. His father and mother and Touch the Clouds were somewhere out on the plains.

Before him loomed the *Astoria*. Zach stroked the oars quietly so as not to draw the attention of those above. Voices and laughter drifted down, and craning his neck, he saw passengers moving about on the hurricane deck. He did not see anyone on the lower deck.

Pulling in the oars, Zach let the rowboat drift against the hull. It scraped and came to a stop.

Steamboats were built low to the water. They had to be. Their shallow draft enabled them to navigate the Mississippi and Missouri Rivers even when those waterways were at their lowest levels. To get on board, Zach only had to balance on the rowboat's seat, stretch his arms high over his head, and spring. His fingers closed on the gunwale and he started to pull himself up and over.

Almost too late, Zach noticed two deckhands coming along the main deck. The roustabouts had not noticed him, and he quickly hung over the side to wait for them to pass.

To Zach's consternation, they stopped a few feet away and one asked the other for a light. A lucifer flared, and an acrid scent tingled Zach's nose. For a few seconds he thought he would sneeze, but the urge faded, and when the pair walked on, he swiftly clambered over the side and crouched in the shadows.

Drawing his Bowie, Zach padded aft. The knife was quieter than a pistol. He did not want to kill any of the crew if he could help it, but neither would he let them stand in his way.

He was almost to the main stairway when voices warned him someone was coming, and he flattened behind a stack of logs that would feed the steam engine once the vessel was under way.

A woman and a man strolled around the boiler. Linked

arm in arm, they walked to the rail and the woman leaned on it and sighed.

"Just think, Horace. Tomorrow we leave for New York. Aren't you excited?"

"I still don't see why we couldn't take the stage, Agnes dear. You know how easily I become seasick."

"Oh, posh. The sea air will do you good. You are far too sickly. I wish I had known that when I married you."

"What are you saying?"

"Nothing, Horace. But I really wish you were more robust. A wife wants her man to be manly."

There was more talk, mostly silly bickering. Chafing at the delay, Zach had to lie there and listen to it all. Eventually, Horace was cowed into admitting that he needed more exercise, and the married couple drifted elsewhere.

It made Zach think of Lou. Of how glad he was that she was not a shrew. Of how guilty he felt over leaving her to go after Evelyn alone. But most of all, of how much he loved her and yearned to see her again and hold her in his arms and be reminded of how deeply she loved him.

Shaking himself, Zach rose into a crouch and glided to the main stairway. No one was coming down. He raised his right foot to the third step and was about to put his weight on it when from almost directly under him came a loud snore. Under the stairs lay a man in the clothes of a roustabout, as the deckhands were called, curled up on his side, fast asleep.

Zach's father had been on a steamboat once or twice, and Zach remembered him saying that deckhands had a hard life. They toiled all day and night for little pay and lousy food. They were not given bunks to sleep in, but had to content themselves with whatever nook or cranny was handy when they were permitted to take breaks.

Now here lay a roustabout mere feet away. Zach had to get up the stairs. It was the only way to the hurricane deck, and from there to the wheelhouse. He lifted his foot to the third step, hoping it wouldn't creak, and balanced precariously on the edge before steadying himself.

The deckhand went on snoring.

Zach went to climb higher. Suddenly, the snoring stopped. He glanced down and saw the roustabout stir. The man rolled onto his back and smacked his lips and muttered something.

Motionless, Zach waited for him to continue his slumber, but without warning the deckhand blinked and sat up and scratched the whiskers on his chin. Abruptly rising from under the stairs, he stretched and yawned.

Zach was a statue. The roustabout's back was to him, and it might be that the man would walk off without noticing him. But he should have known fate would not be so kind. For the very next moment, the roustabout turned.

"What the hell? Who are you?"

Smiling, Zach stepped to the stair rail and said, "I'm a passenger." As he moved, he switched his grip on the Bowie from the hardwood hilt to the flat of the steel blade. "You wouldn't happen to know where the toilets are, would you?"

"Sure," the roustabout said, and turning, he pointed aft. "This must be your first time on a steamboat, or you would know they're always at the stern."

"So I have heard," Zach said, and brought the hilt of the Bowie crashing down on top of the man's head. He thought he might have to hit him again, but one blow sufficed. The deckhand's legs buckled and he collapsed, senseless.

Quickly bounding down, Zach slid his hands under the man's shoulders and dragged him under the stairs. A glance assured him no one had seen or heard. In long bounds he reached the hurricane deck. Several passengers were on the starboard side, gaily chatting. Angling to port,

Zach raced the length of the passenger compartments. As he passed one a door opened and a heavyset man with a bushy mustache nearly blundered into his path. Swerving, Zach reached the short flight of stairs to the wheelhouse. He had made no more sound than the wind, and the figure at the top of the stairs did not realize he was there.

As silently as a stalking mountain lion, Zach scaled the stairs and slipped up behind Captain Dover. Jabbing the tip of his Bowie against Dover's neck, he warned, "Not a sound or you die."

The captain stiffened and raised his arms as if to show he would not resist, then jerked his head back and bellowed, "All hands on deck! Intruder on board!"

Chapter Three

Evelyn King had never been so sad. In all her thirteen going on fourteen years, she had never felt so miserable. Never felt as if she wanted to curl up into a ball and cry and cry and cry until there were no tears left.

Her eyes watered as she glumly leaned forward in her chair and placed her chin in her hands. She wished she were back with her father and mother in their cabin high in the Rockies. She wished she had never gone to Kansas, never met Athena Borke, never been taken against her will.

But she *had* been, and as her mother liked to say, people must deal with things as they were and not as they would like them to be. She must deal with the situation. She must come up with a way to escape and then find her way back to her family, the many miles and dangers notwithstanding.

But it was hard, so very hard. When she was first abducted, she had been fired with hope and zeal. She knew, just knew, that someone would come to rescue her. Her parents, Zach, Uncle Shakespeare, *someone*. But as the days dragged and no one came, her hope dwindled, her zeal faded.

Against her will, Evelyn had been hauled from Kansas to New Orleans. Now Athena Borke was taking her to Paris by way of New York City. *Paris, France.* Half a world away from the world she knew. She would be adrift among strangers, held prisoner in a foreign country where she could expect no help and no mercy. The thought made her shiver with fear.

Evelyn was trying to be brave. She was trying to live as her folks had taught her over the years. She must never give up. She must always remember that where there was life there was hope. She must think of hardships as challenges to be overcome. But thinking all that and doing it were two different things.

There was a sound outside the locked cabin door. Evelyn dabbed at her eyes and sat up just as the latch rasped and in walked Athena Borke carrying a silver tray with a bowl and a plate of food.

"I thought you always have your hired help wait on me," Evelyn said.

"Spare me your childish barbs, girl," Athena said, depositing the tray on the table. "Nothing you say will hurt my feelings. Just as nothing will change my mind about Paris." She lifted the lid to the bowl. "Look here. I paid extra for the cook to whip this up. Potato soup with bread and butter, and a slice of apple pie for dessert."

"Am I supposed to thank you?"

Athena was across the room in a twinkling and raised her hand to slap Evelyn's face. Instead, slowly lowering it, she said, "No. I refuse to lose my temper. I refuse to give you the satisfaction of gloating about how vile a person I am." Smoothing her black dress, she claimed the other chair. "We need to talk, you and I. By this time tomorrow, we will be well on our way to New York, and I want you to understand your part in the scheme of things."

"What is there to understand?" Evelyn asked. "I am your captive, and if I do not do as you say you will kill me."

"I haven't hurt you yet, have I?" Athena countered. "Other than a few smacks now and again to make you behave?" In the next breath she said, "That is not to say Carlos or Mateo wouldn't do terrible things to you if I told them to. They are extremely loyal to me. I took them out of the gutter when they were boys no older than you and gave them a taste of a life they had never known."

"They are killers," Evelyn said.

Athena's haughty features twisted in amusement. "You say that as if you know it to be undisputed fact."

"I do."

Laughing lightly, Athena crossed her legs and placed her hands on her knee. "Come now, little one. You are a child. You know nothing of killing and killers and the like. Admit it."

Evelyn struggled to control her temper. She had never been like her brother, never prone to tantrums at the slightest provocation. She always thought it was because she was more levelheaded. She always thought she was immune. But in recent days she had found her temper flaring time and again. She had learned that she could get as mad as Zach or anyone else, and she was mad now. But she did not let on. It would only amuse Athena Borke more.

"No reply, child? Where is that tart tongue?"

"You're the one who thinks she knows so much but knows so little," Evelyn said. "I was raised in the wilds. I have seen a bear kill a horse and a mountain lion kill deer. I have seen a bobcat kill a bird and a hawk kill a snake. I have seen a raccoon kill a frog and a coyote kill a grouse."

"What does that—?" Athena Borke began.

"Let me finish, if you please," Evelyn said. "I have seen my father kill game. I have seen him kill men who were trying to kill us. I have seen my mother kill animals for the supper pot and enemies who were trying to rub out our family. I have seen my brother kill elk and buffalo and men who were out to slit our throats."

Again Athena tried to interrupt. "All that is quite fascinating, but—"

"I am still not done. I have lived for months at a time with my mother's people, the Shoshones. I have seen their warriors count coup on Piegans who raided their village. I have seen war between two tribes, with men killing men until the ground ran red with blood. I have seen all this and much more." Evelyn paused. "So do not sit there and tell me I do not know about killing and killers. I have seen more of it than you ever will, and I am only half your age." She mentioned that last bit because she knew how vain Athena was about her looks and her age.

"Aren't you the little snit."

Evelyn smiled and said, "Carlos and Mateo are killers. Just like your other servant, Largo, the one my brother killed."

Athena flushed red. "Don't remind me. I owe your accursed family for another life. Largo was my favorite. I was quite fond of him. More fond than you can imagine."

"You were lovers," Evelyn said.

For the first time since they met, Athena Borke was momentarily speechless with surprise. Then: "Can it be I have misjudged you? Can it be you are not the young innocent I thought?"

Evelyn mimicked the woman's own mocking laughter. "You are older than me, but you are the one who knows nothing."

"Have a care, infant."

"Or what? You will sic the twins on me?" Evelyn was enjoying herself. "Let me tell you more. We often go to visit my mother's people, as I said. When we do, we spend days and sometimes weeks in a lodge with another family. Sometimes with two or three families. It is how Indians do things."

"So?" Athena snapped.

"So when a man and a woman want to do what men and women do, they do it right there in the lodge with everyone else around them. One night when I was six, some strange sounds woke me up. My mother's brother and his wife were under a buffalo robe, and the robe was moving, and she was making the sounds. So you see," Evelyn smiled sweetly, "I know about love and lovers, too."

For the longest while, Athena Borke was quiet. Then an odd sort of grin twisted her mouth. "Yes, I think I have misjudged you. You are more worldly in certain respects than I was at your age. But you are also naive. You trusted me when you shouldn't have, and look at where you are now."

"My father likes to say that a person never makes friends if they aren't friendly," Evelyn said.

"Ah, yes. The inestimable Nate King. I have heard so much about him. How his reputation is second to none. How he is a man of his word and has never wronged another human being." Athena laid the sarcasm on thick. "It makes you wonder how someone so noble ever produced someone as despicable as your brother."

Evelyn had been holding her temper in check just fine, but now it boiled like hot water on a stove. "All this because you hate him."

"*Yes, I hate him!*" Athena rasped, rising out of her chair with her fists clenched and her teeth bared. "I hate him as I have never hated anyone. He killed my brothers! I will see him suffer for that. Taking you was only the first step. Before I am through, he will get down on his knees and plead for my mercy."

"Not Zach," Evelyn said. "He might slit your throat, but he will never beg."

"We'll see about that. Now eat your supper." Athena turned to the door but stopped when yelling broke out on the upper deck and a loud commotion ensued. She yanked the door open. Outside, Carlos and Mateo were patiently waiting. "Go see what that is about," she commanded.

One ran off. Evelyn thought it was Mateo, but she could not be sure. They were so much alike it was uncanny.

A shot rang through the night, followed by the pounding of feet and what might be the thud of blows. Carlos had one hand under his jacket. Athena was listening intently to the racket.

So was Evelyn. She could not quite make sense of the words. One man seemed to be shouting the same thing over and over.

People were scurrying past the cabin. Some were running toward the commotion; others were running away from it.

The next moment Mateo was there, whispering into Athena Borke's ear. Athena glanced sharply at Evelyn, then whispered to Mateo and Carlos and closed the door. "We're leaving. Get one of the shawls I bought you."

"Where are we going?" Evelyn had resigned herself to spending the next week cooped up in the cabin, because that was exactly what Athena Borke had told her would be the case.

"Just get the shawl, and be quick about it."

Evelyn recognized that tone. It was Athena's "do it now or else" tone, as she liked to call it. The tone Athena used one evening when she said to take a bath. Evelyn had refused. Not that she did not need one. But she was tired of being bossed around, tired of having to do everything Athena said.

Athena had turned to Carlos—at least Evelyn thought it was Carlos, but she could not tell the brothers apart—and Carlos had turned to her and slapped her so hard, she thought her jaw would break. He wasn't done. With Athena standing back and grinning, Carlos beat her black and blue. He did not strike her on the face again or anywhere the bruises would show.

When he was done, Evelyn lay on the floor quivering in fury. Athena Borke assumed she was gravely hurt and instructed Carlos to leave her be. The pain lingered for days. It had been humiliating, and Evelyn would never forget it.

"Didn't you hear me?" Athena said, brooking no delay.

"I heard you," Evelyn sulked, and went to the closet. The shawl was in a leather bag Athena had bought her, an expensive bag that cost more than most people earned in six months. But Athena always had to have the best, even the best clothes for someone she was planning to kill.

Evelyn wasn't fooled. Athena had promised repeatedly to eventually release her, but Evelyn didn't believe it. There would come a day when she was no longer of any use, and that would be the day Mateo or Carlos or both would finish what Carlos—or was it Mateo?—had started.

"I said to hurry up."

Wrapping the blue shawl about her shoulders, Evelyn scooted to the door. The commotion outside was louder than before. She heard a man scream, heard another swear lustily.

"The deck is crowded, mistress," one of the twins said in the lilting accent both had. "It will slow us down."

"You will not let that happen," Athena Borke said. "Do what is necessary to get me off this boat."

"Whatever we must?" the other twin asked.

"I will deal with the consequences, Mateo. Trust me, faithful one. Have I ever let you down?"

"No, mistress, you have not."

Evelyn noticed that Mateo had a small scar on his chin, a scar she had not noticed previously. It had left a tiny indentation. She glanced at the other twin, whose chin was round and smooth. "Finally," she said aloud.

Carlos threw the door wide and they charged out, the twins in the lead, Athena behind them pulling Evelyn after her. The narrow passage was choked with people streaming toward the main stairway. Passengers, for the most part, although Evelyn glimpsed a man with a white apron who might be the cook and another in a seaman's jacket with blood streaming from his nose.

The commotion came from the boiler deck. Evelyn twisted and tried to see what was going on, but the people blocked her view. Suddenly, Athena smacked her shoulder and jerked the shawl up over her head.

"Don't look back again or I will have Carlos carry you."

At a nod from Athena, the twins forced their way through the press—not carefully and politely, but savagely and violently. They laid about them with their fists and their feet, hitting and kicking anyone and everyone in their mistress's path. Men, women, children fell to the deck bleeding and broken. Some of the men fought back, but the twins were masters at what they did best, and what they did best was hurt people.

Evelyn could barely bear to look. She saw an elderly lady fall with her mouth pulped, saw a girl not much older than she was cry out and slump with her arm bent at an unnatural angle.

"Faster!" Athena urged. "He must not spot us!"

He? Evelyn thought, and a ray of hope flared. She glanced back, not caring one whit if Athena caught her, and hopped up and down in a bid to see over those behind her. But all she saw were more passengers and crew.

Then they reached the stairs and the twins pushed and shoved, clearing a path with their customary flair for mayhem. Athena nearly yanked Evelyn off her feet, she was moving so fast.

The main deck was not as crowded. Evelyn was whisked to the gangplank. As she started down, a gust of wind whipped the shawl from her head, and when she twisted to grab it, she saw the boiler deck. At last the commotion was explained. Her heart leaped into her throat and she cupped a hand to her mouth.

"Zach! It's me! I'm here! Over here!"

Chapter Four

When Zach King was fourteen, he visited Bent's Fort in the company of his father and Shakespeare McNair. While the older men were swapping tall tales with Jim Bridger—Bridger's account of the time he explored California and discovered petrified trees filled with petrified birds warbling petrified songs was one of Zach's favorites—Zach ambled about the post taking in the sights.

A party of freighters bound for Santa Fe were stocking up on supplies. Among them were three men fresh from the East. Only slightly older than Zach, they eyed him with open scorn as he strolled past, and one had the gall to say, "As I live and breathe. Take a gander at this, boys. I do believe we've found us a half-breed."

"Sure looks like one to me," said the second, whose nose was bent from a break long ago that did not mend properly.

"If there's anything I hate worse than Indians," commented the third, "it has to be 'breeds. I mean, what kind of white man would bed a squaw?"

Zach had felt himself grow hot with anger. His parents

were always telling him to turn the other cheek when bigotry reared its vicious head, as it often did. But he did not have his father's patience or his mother's understanding nature. When someone insulted him, his natural inclination was to pound them into the ground. Still, he had tried his best and taken a few more steps when the first one made a comment that no man worthy of manhood could let pass.

"I've heard squaws are filthy with lice and fleas, and they don't take baths but once a year. If at all."

Zach's legs turned of their own accord and he stood before them, his Hawken in the crook of his arms. "Apologize."

"How's that again, 'breed?" the one with the bent nose responded. "Are you talking to us?"

"Say you are sorry for insulting my mother."

The three glanced at one another and laughed. "The hell we will," the third declared. "Go away, boy, while you still can."

"My mother is the sweetest lady I know. I won't stand for you talking about her that way."

"Hell, 'breed," the first spat scornfully, "we were talking about squaws in general, but if you want to bring your mother into this, it's fine by us."

They laughed again, and now Zach was boiling inside, but he masked it by smiling and saying, "Say you are sorry, or else."

"Or else what?" the third one countered. "You'll huff and puff and throw a fit? Go right ahead. It would be something to see."

They laughed some more, and something inside of Zach snapped. He drove the stock of his rifle into the gut of the one with the bent nose, pivoted, and caught the first one across the knee with a downward sweep of the barrel. Then the last one leaped and tackled him and brought him down, and suddenly all three were on him, pinning his arms and cursing and flailing their fists. They were too heavy to throw off. Blows rained on his head and shoulders. They might well have beaten him senseless except that a shadowy shape loomed out of the sun and the three were flung every which way as if they weighed no more than empty flour sacks.

Zach blinked in the glare and said, "Thanks, Pa."

Nate King reached down to help him up. "I can't leave you alone for two minutes, can I?" He said it lightheartedly, but his eyes held a hint of reproach.

"They started it," Zach said.

"No, you did when you threatened them," Nate replied. "Never threaten someone unless you can carry through. It will only make them mad, and they might do something rash."

Standing on the wheelhouse deck as the steamboat captain bellowed his warning, Zach was reminded of his father's advice.

Zach had told Dover not to make a peep or he would die, but he could not carry out the threat. He needed Dover alive to tell him which cabin Athena Borke was in. He had a notion to force Dover there at knifepoint and trick Borke into opening the door at Dover's request.

Maybe the captain had sensed he was bluffing. Or maybe Dover was genuinely brave. Regardless, roustabouts converged on the run from all over the ship. Within moments, four were at the foot of the stairs.

"Now what?" Captain Dover gloated. "You've put yourself in a pickle, King. Kill me and you'll never make it off the *Astoria* alive."

"All I want is Athena Borke."

"You won't get to her through me," Dover said. "She's paid good money to seal my lips, and I intend to give her her money's worth."

30

Unwittingly, the captain had done Zach a favor. Until that moment, he could not be entirely sure Borke was on board. All he had to go on were snippets of talk overheard in a waterfront bar. But now he knew she was. Which meant Evelyn was there, too, and nothing and no one would stop him from reaching her. "She's kidnapped my sister."

"I suspected something wasn't quite right," Dover admitted, "but I don't meddle in the private affairs of my passengers."

"Evelyn is just a girl." Zach sought to prey on the other's sympathy. "All I want is to take her home."

"How touching," Captain Dover said, then gestured at the swelling ranks of deckhands. "But you have a more immediate problem. How are you going to get off my ship without having your skull caved in?"

Zach wagged the Bowie. "I know how to use this."

"And my men know how to use their dirks and daggers," Captain Dover warned. "I've got the toughest crew to ever travel the Mississippi, and that is saying a lot."

Zach was aware of the well-deserved reputation roustabouts had for being as tough as iron nails and as prickly as porcupines. It was said they would fight at the drop of a hat, and they would drop the hat. He tried a final appeal: "All I want is my sister."

"Haven't you been listening? There's no way in hell I'm turning her over to you. She doesn't mean a thing to me."

Zach's temper surged. His sister was as gentle a soul as ever lived, and one of the people he loved most in the world. For weeks worry had gnawed at him like a beaver on a tree, worry so potent he couldn't sleep at night, and rarely ate. To have her life so callously thrown in his face was more than he could bear. "She means everything to me," he said, and struck Dover across the temple with the Bowie's hardwood hilt.

31

The captain folded at the waist, and a cry of outrage went up from below. Several roustabouts leaped to their employer's aid.

"You want him?" Zach asked, and shoved.

Dover was still conscious and squawked as he tumbled down the stairs. He clutched at a rail to arrest his fall, but he could not get a good enough grip. Cartwheeling end over end, he crashed into three deckhands and all four wound up at the bottom in a tangled heap, with only two of them still moving.

More roustabouts started up the stairs. Some had knives. Some had short clubs. Others came running up to reinforce those already there.

Zach had two options. He could fight or he could vault over the side to the boiler deck and from there reach shore. But if he fled, he lost his best chance to rescue Evelyn since her abduction, and he would be damned if he would desert her. Accordingly, he charged down the stairs into the waiting weapons of the roustabouts.

A burly deckhand slashed a dagger at his gut. Sidestepping, he flicked the Bowie twice, and at each stroke blood welled on the man's wrist. The glittering dagger dropped from fingers gone numb. Swearing savagely, the man pressed his wrist to his side and turned to run, but he had nowhere to go. The lower steps were blocked by others. The roustabout tripped and fell headlong, taking several of his fellows with him.

"Kill the son of a bitch!" someone hollered.

Slashing right and left, Zach waded into them. In the narrow space between the rails, they could only come at him one or two at a time. Many were bigger than he was, but his long blade more than made up for their greater reach.

A Bowie in the hands of a skilled knife fighter was as fearsome a weapon as any ever invented. Named after the famed adventurer of the same name, Bowies varied in size and shape depending on the manufacturer. In England, more than sixty firms were engaged in producing Bowie knives as fast as they could fill orders. In America, factories in Baton Rouge, Shelburne Falls, Baltimore, and Philadelphia strove to meet the high demand.

Some Bowies were single-edged. Some were double-edged. Purists claimed that a certain size and shape qualified as a real Bowie and all the rest were impostors, but that did not stop companies from churning out knives that bore little or no resemblance to the legendary knife carried by its famous owner.

Zach's Bowie was fifteen and a half inches long and three inches across at the hilt, with a curved point. Doubled-edged at the tip, it was single-edged the rest of its length. The hilt was hickory. A bronze guard and bronze cap at the end of the hilt added a flash of color. Heavy and razor-sharp, it could cleave an arm or a skull with supremely lethal ease.

Not that Zach wanted to kill anyone. He would rather be allowed to go about his quest in peace, but the roustabouts were out for blood. He had hurt their captain, and they were determined that he pay.

Another deckhand lunged, thrusting low. Zach avoided the cold steel and retaliated in kind. His descending stroke caught the man across the left shoulder, shearing through fabric and flesh to bone.

Screeching in anguish, the man threw himself backward, blood spurting in a fine scarlet mist.

"Get him!" a roustabout at the back of the pack brayed.

A few more steps and Zach would reach the deck. Blade rang off blade as he countered attempt after attempt to bring him down. His next stab opened a neck. Then a tall roustabout reared, wielding an ax. Where the man got it from, Zach would never know. It swept at his face. Ducking, Zach sliced a furrow over a foot long along the man's ribs.

"Stop him, damn it!" The strident cry sounded like Captain Dover's voice.

Shoes pounded the deck. The vessel was crawling with more hands than Zach imagined. Those nearest were trying to be the one to lay him low. Bedlam reigned, with Zach at the center of the whirlwind.

The uproar they were making was loud enough to be heard on shore. Zach would have a heap of explaining to do if the law butted in. Of even more concern was the possibility Athena Borke would overhear the commotion and come to investigate. An enemy forewarned was an enemy forearmed, and Zach dearly desired to take Borke by surprise.

Crouching, Zach leaped at the roustabouts, swinging his Bowie. They scrambled back, frantic in their haste, and he gained the boiler deck. He bore right, thinking to retrace his steps along the passageway to the main stairs and from there reach the lower deck, but now the roustabouts had room to move and they did not move back when he rushed them. They met his charge head-on. Their expressions showed that they were confident their superior numbers would prevail.

Passengers were watching from the fringes of the deck. Two young women in fancy dresses pointed at Zach and whispered excitedly. To them it was great entertainment until he broke toward the off-side rail, swinging the Bowie in a frenzy that forced the roustabouts back. Then the women screamed and hastened down the passageway.

Zach paused when the roustabouts drew back beyond the reach of his Bowie. They had tasted of his skill and were wary of him.

"Be sensible, 'breed!" hollered one with a barrel of a body. "Throw down your pigsticker while you can!"

"I want my sister," Zach said.

"Who?" The man glanced at Captain Dover, who was

on his hands and knees and unsteadily trying to rise. "What is he talking about, sir?"

"Nothing that need concern you, Kochinka" was Dover's harsh reply. "Get at him, all of you! A hundred dollars to whoever brings him low!"

"Is that alive or dead?" wondered one of the river rats.

"Any way you can do it," Captain Dover said.

They swarmed forward, four and five abreast. Zach parried and twisted, stabbed and countered. He did not dare slow down, did not dare stop. At any moment he half expected a searing sensation in the back or between his ribs.

By now Zach had strayed far enough from the steps that the roustabouts had him completely surrounded. His only option was to fight his way out, and the consequences be damned. "Whoever doesn't want to die," he said, "had better leave." He figured two or three would heed, but he should have known better.

"Brave words, boy," one spat, "for someone who doesn't have a snowball's chance in hell of making it off this boat alive."

Zach had done what little he could. He tore into them anew, swinging the Bowie in a berserk fury. A knife almost as big rose to meet his, and he battered it aside like an inconsequential twig. A dirk sheared at his groin and he flattened its wielder with an uppercut. Someone lanced a butcher knife at his chest. He avoided it with the width of a cat's whisker to spare and, out of instinct more than design, sank the Bowie to its hilt in the man's side.

To a man, the roustabouts froze. So far they had been spared serious harm, or worse. Many had been cut and some had been stabbed, but no one had died. Mouths slack, they watched as the man Zach had stabbed pitched to the deck, briefly convulsed, and gave up the ghost.

"He's killed Charley!"

"Kill the bastard!"

Hate filled their eyes, hate and bloodlust. At a bellow from a man bent over Captain Dover, the deckhands closed in from every point of the compass at once.

Ordinarily, that would be enough to overwhelm just about anyone. But Zach had fought in clashes between the Shoshones and other tribes involving large numbers. He was no stranger to battle, no novice at dealing death and mayhem. As grim as death, he met their rush. They were many, but he was lightning quick. They had the advantage, but that only made him more desperate.

Just then, someone screamed his name.

Someone whose voice he recognized.

Chapter Five

Zach King had been searching for his sister for a number of weeks. He had scoured the trail from Kansas to New Orleans without success. It was only a question of time, he had told himself over and over to bolster his confidence. Since learning Evelyn was on the *Astoria*, he expected to find her before the night was out. Yet when the moment came, when she screamed his name and he whirled to behold her being whisked down the gangplank by Athena Borke and a pair of swarthy men in dark clothes, he was so startled, he turned to stone.

"Evelyn!" Relief washed over him in a flooding wave. Zach took a step toward the shore side of the steamboat and promptly had to dodge a roustabout who speared a knife at his throat.

What little control Zach had left snapped. He had to reach Evelyn and he had to do it right then. Whipping the Bowie in an arc, he sliced the roustabout's throat from ear to ear. A crimson spray spattered the deck as he skipped past the falling body and into the waiting blades of more adversaries.

If they would not get out of his way, they would suffer. Zach was out to kill. He deflected a dagger, opened a wrist, blocked a butcher knife, sheared through an arm. Curses and cries rose in a crescendo. He barely heard them. His own blood was pounding so fiercely that the hammering of his pulse eclipsed all else.

The roustabouts hemmed him, refusing to give him a sliver of headway. Whatever else might be said of their lusty, rowdy ways, they were not cowards. They threw themselves at him with a bloodthirsty abandon he might have regarded as refreshing under different circumstances. He had a bloodthirsty nature himself, or so he had been told, and these were men whose fighting spirits were reflections of his own. But they stood between him and his sister, and he would send them to their white man's hell before he would let them keep him from her.

A skinny deckhand came at him swinging a knife even longer than his. Zach heard the blade whisk past his ear and the next instant sank his Bowie into the deckhand's chest. The man fell, opening a path to the side, a path filled by more roustabouts before Zach could take two steps.

Dover was screeching something about not letting him escape. Passengers were pouring down the passageway to the main stairs and from there onto the main deck, where they stopped, thinking themselves out of harm's reach, and gaped. Their lapse in judgment was borne home by a roustabout who drew a small pistol and fired at Zach's back from a range of less than five feet. By rights the slug should have cored Zach between his shoulder blades. But at the same split second the roustabout fired, Zach shifted to avoid the stroke of another man's knife. The lead meant for him hit an onlooker on the main deck, who wailed like a four-year-old as he toppled, inciting a new panic.

The roustabout retreated from the melee to reload.

Drawing one of his own pistols, Zach pointed it at the deckhands in front of him. He should have done it sooner. They melted from his path like leaves blown by a tempest. Blades were their preferred weapon of choice; the only one with a gun was the one reloading.

Racing to the rail, Zach whirled to hold them at bay. The quickest way to reach the main deck was to swing over the rail and drop, but to do that, Zach must wedge the pistol under his belt and slide the Bowie into its sheath to free his hands. Unarmed, he would be overpowered by the roustabouts should they elect to rush him.

There was only way to dissuade them. Zach shot one. He aimed at the man's thigh and put a hole in it as big around as an apple. Shoving the Bowie into its sheath, he made as if to draw his other pistol. The roustabouts scattered.

In a blur, Zach spun and shoved the spent pistol under his belt and gripped the top rail, vaulting over the side. At the apex of his leap, he whipped his entire body around, changing his grip on the rail as he turned, and swung in and down, dropping lightly onto the main deck only a few yards from the gangplank.

Too late, Zack saw panicked passengers streaming toward him. His sudden appearance stopped them cold. Those in the rear ran into those in front, driving them toward him. To keep them back, he resorted to the Bowie, which had the magical effect of scattering them like sheep.

"Zach! Zach! Help me!" His sister was being pulled toward a carriage by Athena Borke. She resisted with every sinew in her small frame, but the woman in black was too strong.

"*Evelyn!*" Zach's voice did not sound like his own. He bounded onto the gangplank but got no farther.

Two swarthy figures in dark suits were midway down,

their intentions as plain as the slim knives they held low. They were twins. More of Borke's hirelings, Zach guessed, killers working for her under the guise of manservants like the one he had killed in Kansas. He did not ask them to get out of his way. He did not try to reason with them. He raised the Bowie and rushed them, but was given pause by the crack of a shot from the vicinity of the carriage.

Alain de Fortier was on his knees, doubled over. A smoking pistol in her hand, Athena Borke was about to climb into the carriage. Evelyn's legs were jutting from the open door, but they were not moving.

Blind panic seized Zach. He was sure Alain had been shot, not Evelyn, but something had happened to her or she would not be so still. Heedless of his welfare, he sprang down the gangplank, only to stop abruptly when the sinister pair in the dark suits came at him with the superb swiftness of mountain cats. Their knives slashed in concert, and it was all Zach could do to parry their thrusts.

Out of the corner of his eye, Zach glimpsed Athena Borke scrambling into the carriage and the driver raising his whip. In rising desperation, he feinted at the twin on his right while gliding left, his shoulder low to absorb the shock of slamming into the other one. But he misjudged the other's reflexes. A foot hooked under his own and the gangplank rose to meet his cheek. He thought for sure they would sink their knives into his back, but when he heaved onto the balls of his feet, they were at the bottom of the gangplank, running toward the carriage.

Zach bolted after them. The carriage was in motion, moving rapidly away, the door still open. He reached the street going flat out and poured on every iota of speed he could muster.

The twins caught up to the carriage. Never breaking stride, first one and then the other grabbed the edge of the door and swung lithely inside. The door slammed shut and the face of one appeared in the window. A mocking smirk lit his cruel features.

"No!" Zach roared, his legs flying. But it was not enough. The carriage came to the intersection and swept around it in a medley of rattling wheels and pounding hooves. When he reached the intersection, it was two blocks away. He could still catch it if he had a horse, but the only one in sight was almost as far off as the carriage. "Evelyn," Zach said softly.

A sound behind him made Zach whirl, but it was Alain, his left arm stiff at his side.

"The bitch shot me, *mon ami*."

"I must go after them. Keep up if you can." Zach jogged north and de Fortier fell into step beside him. His friend's face was ghostly pale, and he held on to the Hawken with an effort. Zach snatched it from his grasp.

"I was a fool," Alain said. "But old habits die hard, and I am first and foremost a gentleman. I asked her to please place her hands in the air, and she pulled a derringer on me."

"I warned you not to take her lightly." Bitter experience had taught Zach that Athena Borke was as deadly as any man who ever lived. Like her brothers, she had no scruples, no conscience. Anyone who stood in her way was fodder to be disposed of. Where most others would be held to account by the rigid arm of the law, her wealth protected her. In white society wealth was power, and she was as clever as a fox at using hers to devious ends.

Out of a side street appeared a horseman. Zach veered toward him, and Alain instantly grabbed his shoulder.

"What are you up to? If it is what I think it is, you mustn't. Stealing a horse is not a small offense."

Shrugging loose, Zach growled, "I will not lose Evelyn again." To have been so close and then be foiled was tearing at his insides like a red-hot fireplace poker. The carriage was no longer in sight, but with luck he could find it again.

"You cannot help your sister behind bars."

"Don't try to stop me," Zach said, then realized that his shirt, where his friend had touched it, was wet. Alain's hand was caked with blood and large drops were falling from his fingers. It was like a slap to the face. In his rabid concern for Evelyn, he had given no thought to Alain's condition. "How bad are you hit?"

"Bad" was the reply, and Alain faltered and slowed. "I am afraid I cannot be of further use at the moment." Groaning, he closed his eyes and buckled at the knees.

Zach caught him and half carried him over near a lit window. Quickly, he peeled back Alain's cape and shirt to find that the bullet had caught him high on the left side of the chest, dangerously near the heart.

A shriek of frustration and fury nearly tore from Zach's throat. If he left Alain there, Alain would surely die. But if he helped him, finding Evelyn would be that much harder.

A clacking noise rattled the night from the direction of the *Astoria*. Zach remembered that the police beat on sidewalks and walls with their nightsticks to signal one another. They might already be searching for someone answering his description.

"Damn," Zach said, and with his rifle under one arm, he lifted Alain and ducked down a dark side street. Part of him railed at what he was doing. Part of him howled and cursed and did not relent until, nearly twenty minutes later, the lights of the hospital sparkled invitingly. His legs ached and his lower back had a severe cramp, but he did not set Alain down until he had shoved through the wide door and a nurse came running at his call.

"His name is Alain de Fortier. He has been shot." Zach did not say more. They would find out in time. The police would question Alain, but it was doubtful they would arrest him.

A doctor and aides hurried down the hall. As they clustered about Alain, checking his condition, Zach backed to the door and slipped quietly out into the night. At the end of the block, he stopped under a shadowed overhang and asked himself, *What now?* What would Athena Borke do? Where would he find her? She might book passage on another steamboat bound for New York City. The newspaper printed long lists of departure times for every vessel. His first step, then, was to buy one.

As Zach prowled the city's narrow, winding byways looking for a street hawker, a deep sadness afflicted him. Sometimes it seemed as if Providence itself were conspiring against him. Every time he got close to Evelyn, she was snatched away. He remembered her upturned face at the dock, filled with hope and love, and he withered inside like a dying plant. He had failed her yet again.

Zach regretted running off so impulsively on his wife. He could use Louisa now. Her clear head and sharp mind were equal to any problem. She would know how to go about finding Borke in half the time he could.

Hunting a human was not like hunting an animal. Deer, elk, buffalo, they all had their habits, and a hunter who knew those habits could always find them. Humans were creatures of habit, too, but not to the same degree. Even less so when they knew they were being hunted. Athena Borke would do all she could to throw him off the scent. She had a genius for always doing the unexpected, for always staying one step ahead.

Zach tried to think of what that might be. Since he was expecting her to try to slip out of the city on a ship, maybe she would travel by land. Or maybe she would simply rent a dwelling under an assumed name, as she had done in Kansas, and lie low until he had given up. In which case she would be lying low forever, since he would never stop searching.

Unbidden, the image of Evelyn's legs jutting from the carriage filled Zach's mind, and icy dread slowed the blood in his veins. If anything had happened to her, if Athena Borke had harmed her, Borke would suffer as few others ever had. He didn't care that she was a woman. She deserved to die anyway for what she had done. He wouldn't hesitate a second to slit her throat or put a slug into her.

Zach knew his father would say that a man must never let his animal passions get the better of him, but Zach couldn't help it if he had been born with a fiery temper. He tried to control it, he truly did, but ever since he could remember, when his anger turned to rage he was swept along on a flood of violent emotion, as helpless to resist as a leaf in a gale.

His temper had brought all this about. When he had learned that Athena's brother, Artemis, was trying to incite a war between the Shoshones and the Crows, when he discovered Artemis was selling liquor to the Shoshones and cheating them out of furs and horses, his fury had been boundless. He always considered himself more Shoshone than white, and was proud to be counted as one of his mother's people. To see an unscrupulous trader use them for greedy ends had been more than he could bear.

Stifling a yawn, Zach wearily rubbed his eyes. He had not slept well in months. He had not eaten well, either. It was taking a toll, but he could not be bothered about his health until Evelyn was safe.

A squeal of laughter brought Zach out of his reverie. In his wandering he had come to Canal Street. To his right was the French Quarter, to his left the city's fledgling business district. As the city's main artery, Canal Street was filled with traffic: carriages, phaetons, drays, buggies, riders, pedestrians. Here he need not worry about the police. He was just one face among many.

Or so Zach assumed until he had gone another block. A pair of policemen rounded the corner, and in his haste he nearly bumped into them. He quickly tucked his chin to his chest and started to turn the other way, but his luck had not improved.

The policemen stopped and stared in his direction. The older and stouter of the two gestured. "You there, in the buckskins."

Zach took a step but realized he could not outrun them with them so near. He touched a finger to his chest. "Do you mean me?"

"Yes, you. Who else is wearing buckskins? We would like to have a word with you." And the policeman's hand fell to his pistol.

Chapter Six

Evelyn King had never been afraid of the dark, but she was afraid of it now. All around her was black as pitch. She did not know where she was or how she had got there. She became aware of a sensation of movement. She wasn't moving, but something around her was. Then she heard the unmistakable clatters of wheels and it all came back to her in a vivid rush: seeing Zach, being dragged to the carriage, fighting fiercely to break free and go to him, and being struck across the head by Athena Borke.

With a start, Evelyn opened her eyes. She was slumped in the backseat of a carriage. Beside her was Athena; across from them were the Creole twins, Mateo and Carlos. Evelyn shuddered, for the last she had seen of them, they were on the gangplank awaiting her brother, and if they were there, unharmed, then it must mean her brother was— She could not bring herself to finish the thought. She sat up straighter and felt pain spike her head. Reaching up, she touched a large bump. "Did you have to hit me so hard? And what did you hit me with, anyway?"

"Well, well, well. Look who is back among the living,"

Athena said. "Count your blessings, child. I hit you with a derringer in my hand. I could just as well have shot you, and good riddance, you little nuisance."

Evelyn leaned toward the window. They were winding along a narrow street flanked by elegant homes with balconies. "What about Zach?"

"He is very much alive and well. The police might have him in custody, but I doubt it. He has more lives than a cat, that damn brother of yours."

"They didn't kill him?" Evelyn asked, with a bob of her chin at the twins. Their faces were cold, empty slates.

"They weren't supposed to," Athena said. "Only delay him long enough for us to get away." She smoothed her black dress and fluffed at her hair. "Did you honestly think I would deprive myself of the pleasure of making his life a living hell? He hasn't begun to suffer for what he did."

"You let him live just so you can torment him?" Evelyn had never met anyone so unspeakably wicked.

"Why do you sound surprised? I'm out for revenge, am I not? And revenge is a dish best served piping hot."

"Yet you spared him," Evelyn said. But then, there was much about Athena Borke she did not quite understand.

"I could have had your brother killed long ago. But where is the justice in according him a quick, painless death? He must feel the hurt I have felt. He must feel the misery, the loss. Only after I have hurt him as much as I can will he reap his just deserts for my brothers."

"You keep blaming him, but they started it," Evelyn brought up for the hundredth time. "It was Artemis who made trouble for the Shoshones. It was Phineas who took Zach's wife to get back at him for Artemis's death. All my brother did was stand up for his tribe and his family."

"He's hardly a saint," Athena said harshly. "Your brother is a primitive savage like those Shoshones you keep talking about. All he knows is how to kill. He was raised in the wilderness, so it's no wonder he thinks and acts like a beast. But he's in *my* world now. I set the rules, not him. I will keep him dancing like a puppet on a string for as long as it suits my fancy."

"I hate you," Evelyn said.

"I'm sure you do. I would, were I in your petite shoes. And I have no doubt you will hate me even more when I finally dispose of your brother for good and forever." Athena placed her hand on Evelyn's head, and Evelyn jerked back.

"Don't touch me!"

"Spare me your silly tantrums," Athena said. "Eventually, you will come to appreciate I'm only doing what I must. That if my brothers had killed yours, our roles would be reversed."

"All I know is that you are the meanest woman alive and if I had a gun I would shoot you," Evelyn said.

"I believe you would. We are a lot more alike, you and I, than you'll ever be candid enough to admit."

"We are nothing alike!" Evelyn declared, appalled. She had never in her life gone out of her way to hurt another person.

Athena recited a litany. "You love your brother, I loved mine. You would do anything for him, I would do anything for them. You put family above all else, I do the same. It sure sounds like a lot in common to me."

Evelyn fell silent. They had been through this before. She caught the twins staring at her and demanded, "What are you two looking at?"

"Behave, child," Athena cautioned. "They have not laid a finger on you yet, but that is not to say they won't if you give me cause."

"Aren't you forgetting when Carlos beat me?"

"A lesson, nothing more. I could have had you beaten

48

or whipped any time I chose, but I have spared you out of the kindness of my heart."

Evelyn laughed the older woman to scorn and was rewarded with a flush of anger. "Kind? You don't know the meaning of the word."

"Keep it up and I might change my mind," Athena warned. "I like you, but there are limits as to how far you can push." Settling back into the soft seat, she contemplated the night sky. "The big question now is what to do next? Do I take you to Paris or amend my original plans?"

"Amend them how?" Evelyn asked.

"I tire of all this cat and mouse. Your brother's persistence has become an annoyance I can do without. He has a knack for showing up at the most inconvenient moment. Perhaps it is time to put him in his place. For the hunted to become the hunter, as he might phrase it."

Evelyn did not like the sound of that. "My brother is one of the best hunters in the mountains. He knows all there is to know."

"About the mountains, yes, but look out your window. Those are buildings, not snow-covered peaks. Here I make the rules." Athena idly drummed her fingers on her knee. "I have it. I will set a trap for him. Carlos and Mateo will spring it, and after they are done, your beloved brother will be a shell of his former self."

"How do you mean?"

"There are things worse than death. Maiming, for instance. How mad would you be if I had one of his knees broken? Or perhaps arranged things so he could never have children?"

It took a few seconds for Evelyn to grasp the significance, and revulsion such as she had never known coursed through her. "You wouldn't! That's plain sick!"

"Indians mutilate whites and other Indians all the

time," Athena said. "What I will do to him is no different than if he were captured by the Sioux or the Blackfeet. At least I will leave him alive."

"Just so you can torture him again," Evelyn said bitterly.

"Now you're catching on."

The twins were grinning. Evelyn wished she had a pair of flintlocks. Thanks to her father, she was an excellent shot. During her childhood, he spent hours versing her in how. He even had a rifle custom-made for her by the Hawken brothers.

"Yes, indeed," Athena was saying. "This promises to be highly entertaining. I will, of course, be there when they do it. I want to laugh at him when he is down and rub his nose in his failure."

"You are awful" was all Evelyn could think of to say.

"So I am, and proud of it." Athena laughed merrily. "I haven't enjoyed myself this much since the slums."

"The slums?" Evelyn repeated. "What are they?"

"That's right. You wouldn't know, would you, living at the top of the world as you do? With deer and bears for neighbors?" Athena tittered. "A slum is where the poor live, my dear, in the most wretched squalor. In New York City it is worse than anywhere else, because there are too few good jobs and hordes of immigrants pouring into the country every day. Real estate, in which I like to invest, can be had for a pittance."

"You buy houses for poor people?"

Athena's loudest laugh yet filled the carriage. "Honestly, your naïveté is astounding. I own more than a few tenements, yes, but not out of the goodness of my heart. I own them because they require little upkeep yet bring in many times their worth in rent each year."

Evelyn absorbed that, then said, "The poor people pay you to live in—how did you put it? Squalor?"

"Yes, child. Isn't it delicious? They hand over what little

money they earn for the right to live in rodent-infested apartments with walls so thin, you can always hear what is going on next door. They freeze in the winter and bake in the summer, and they think they are fortunate because they are not living on the street."

"That's terrible," Evelyn summed up her sentiments. No one had ever mentioned this aspect of civilization, not even her father, who once lived in New York City. "How can people let that happen?"

"Because they don't give a damn, little one. All that talk about being your brother's keeper is so much hot wind. When you get right down to it, when you peel away the layers of lies people pretend to live by, no one cares what happens to the other person so long as it does not happen to them."

"That's not true," Evelyn objected. "My mother's people don't live like that. Shoshones care about other Shoshones. They don't do anything that will hurt another member of the tribe. When there isn't enough food, everyone goes hungry. And they all have their own lodges."

"You make it sound utopian," Athena said, "but tell me the truth. Are there rich and poor Shoshones?"

"Some have more horses than others, yes, and some live in bigger lodges than others. But my mother says that's only natural."

"Is it indeed? I submit it's no more natural than rich whites living in mansions while poor whites live in tenements. It's basic human nature, white or red, to want to have it better than everyone else, even if that means some go hungry or live in filthy holes overrun by rats."

Evelyn opened her mouth to argue but closed it again. She did not want to admit it, but her abductor had a point. And what did that say about the state of civilization? She had long envisioned life in the States as the closest thing to perfection on earth, but maybe she was wrong. She had never given much thought to the white world's less savory underbelly. Perhaps it was time she did.

"Look around you," Athena Borke went on. "All these fine spacious homes with gardens and yards and fountains. But you saw with your own eyes how those who live along the waterfront must content themselves with one-room shacks made of planks. It is the same everywhere."

For a long while after that, Evelyn did not say anything. She was too deep in thought, comparing the world she knew, the wilderness, to the world around her. When the carriage came to a stop, she finally raised her head and looked out. "Where are we?" She could not tell much in the darkness.

"At the estate of a friend. His name is Palantine. He and I share certain mutual business interests."

"Real estate?" Evelyn asked.

"No," Athena answered, and smiled enigmatically.

Carlos and Mateo were first out and held the door for their mistress. "Bring her," Athena commanded, and the twins hemmed Evelyn on each side as they climbed marble stairs to an ornate door with a large brass knocker. Athena banged it twice, and the echo ran hollowly through the mansion.

Within seconds a black butler in a white jacket and pants opened the door and grinned broadly. "Miss Borke! Why, wait until my master finds out you are here! He thinks the world of you, you know."

"It will be a pleasure to see him again, James," Athena said, sweeping past with a rustle of her dress. "Fetch him to the parlor, if you please."

Evelyn had never set foot in a house so grand. The walls were polished wood, the ceiling rose to a high vault from which a crystal chandelier was suspended, and the carpet was so soft her feet seemed to sink into it. She hardly noticed as the twins ushered her down the long hall to a room four times as big as the cabin she grew up in, with plush furniture in rich brown hues.

Athena was watching her closely. "So tell me, little one. Would you rather live here or in a hovel?"

"Here," Evelyn said.

"Which proves my point that you are more like me than you are willing to admit," Athena gloated.

Troubled, Evelyn sank into an easy chair with a back so high, her head rose only halfway to the top and her feet did not touch the floor. Mateo stood on one side, Carlos on the other, their slender hands clasped behind their backs, as still as statues. The house itself was so quiet that she heard the ticking of a grandfather clock in the corner.

"If you think this is something," Athena said, "wait until I take you to my villa in France. Or my cotton plantation in South Carolina, bequeathed to me by my dear, departed husband, who died of unknown natural causes." At that, Athena chortled.

The doorway filled with a bear of a man with grayish-blond curly hair and a chest like a barrel. He had a square face, a prominent jaw, and moon-shaped eyes of burning brown. "As I live and breathe!" he declared in a deep voice. "Athena, my dear! I was beginning to think you would never again grace my doorstep with your elegant presence, and that would be a true tragedy."

"My dear Palantine," Athena said, clearly pleased, and held out a hand, which he gently took and pressed to his thick lips. "I do hope you will forgive the intrusion, but I am in a bind and have nowhere else to turn."

"My home, my servants, my very self are at your disposal." Palantine bowed graciously, then noticed Evelyn. His leonine head rose and he sauntered over and took one of her small hands in one of his big ones, as he had taken Athena's. "What have we here, pray tell?" Delicately kissing her knuckles, he purred, "Where did you find such a charming child? Her eyes, her skin, her hair. Please say she is a gift and you are giving her to me to do with her as I please."

"Now, there's an idea," Athena Borke said.

Chapter Seven

The two policemen were bound to know the streets and alleyways better than Zach. Even if he did by some chance elude them, they would signal to other officers for help. That, or they might just shoot him in the back. Word was that the city's officers were a tad too eager to pull the trigger. There were also whispers of widespread corruption. Plastering a smile on his face, he tried a bluff. "How may I be of service?"

His polite manner surprised them. The stout one's bushy eyebrows arched and he looked Zach up and down. "Listen to you. You sound more like a refined gentleman than a 'breed."

That word again. Zach bore the insult and said, "My mother raised me to always be considerate."

The other policeman snorted. "His mother? Did you hear that, Lester? Talk about fresh in from the hills."

"Hush, Toby," Lester said. He still had his hand on his pistol, but some of the flintiness in his expression had faded. "We're looking for someone. There was a disturbance down by the waterfront and a bulletin has been put out on a man wearing buckskins."

Zach held his smile in place. "There must be a couple of hundred frontiersmen in New Orleans right this moment." He was exaggerating, but there were a lot.

Toby answered before Lester could. "Maybe there are, but 'breeds in buckskins are another story, boy. There can't be but a handful. Were you on a ship called the *Astoria* earlier tonight?"

"Never heard of it, sir," Zach lied.

"So you claim" was Toby's retort.

Lester sighed and said, "Let me handle this, will you? I don't interrupt when you're questioning some, do I?"

"Fine. Go ahead."

Zach did not understand why they were sniping at one another, but it could be exploited to his advantage. "I don't mind answering any questions either of you have," he said in the same civil tone.

"You haven't been near the waterfront?" Lester asked.

"No, sir. I just got into New Orleans today from Kansas and I've been taking in the sights. I swear, there are more saloons and taverns here than anywhere in the world. And all the women!"

Lester grinned knowingly. "I remember what it's like being your age. I was only interested in one thing, too." He paused. "But I still need to do my duty. What's your name, son?"

Zach used the first one that popped into his head. "Nate McNair."

"Well, McNair, I'm afraid we'll have to take you in for questioning," Lester said. "If it's any consolation, every half-breed in the city is being brought in. Whatever happened on the *Astoria* has some people in high places in a dither, and they want the one responsible."

"You're taking me to jail?" Again Zach fought down an

urge to bolt. He did not have time for this. Every second he squandered was another second Evelyn spent in Athena Borke's clutches.

"You're not under arrest or anything," Lester said.

"Yet," Toby added.

They moved to each side of him, and Lester gestured. "This way. It's only a few blocks. We won't keep you more than an hour, I should think. We have to send word to headquarters and they'll send the *Astoria*'s captain down to have a look at you."

Zach's gut balled into a knot. Once Captain Dover identified him, they would throw him behind bars and keep him there until his trial. He couldn't let that happen. But he obediently turned and walked in the direction indicated, the Hawken cradled in his arms. It mildly surprised him that they had not relieved him of his weapons, but no sooner did the thought cross his mind than the one called Toby reached around and gripped the rifle's barrel.

"I'll take this if you don't mind, and those pistols, too."

Zach nearly drew one, but Lester was watching him closely and both men had hands on their side arms. Maintaining his innocent act, he smiled and said, "No problem, sir. Here you go." He handed them over and waited for them to ask for his Bowie, but either they hadn't noticed it, partially hidden as it was by his left arm, or they didn't care.

"Keep walking," Toby directed.

At the next corner was a streetlight. Zach walked under it without a second thought and turned right when Toby told him to. Suddenly, the policeman grabbed him by the arm and spun him half around.

"What the hell is this?"

Uncomprehending, Zach glanced down and was as shocked as his escorts. His buckskin shirt was spattered with drops of dry blood. A much larger stain marked where Alain de Fortier's shoulder had pressed against his midriff when he carried Alain to the hospital.

"That's blood!" Lester declared.

Toby trained one of Zach's own pistols on him and cocked it. "I suppose you have no idea how it got there, do you, 'breed?"

Struggling to stay calm, Zach answered, "Sure I do. From a deer I butchered yesterday. I have a tent pitched in the woods west of here, and I've been living off the land." He added as if it were an afterthought, "I don't have a lot of money, so I have to make do as best I can."

"And you expect us to believe you?" Toby took a step back so more space was between them. "How stupid do you think we are?"

"Let's not rush to judgment," Lester said. "It could be just as he says."

Toby swore. "You're always so ready to give trash like this the benefit of the doubt. One of these days, you'll get a blade in the back if you're not careful."

"All I'm saying is that his story could be true," Lester defended himself. "Woodsmen like to have the stars over their heads at night, not a roof. My grandfather was that way."

Zach gauged the distance to Toby and opted not to do anything for the moment. When ordered to go on, he hummed to himself to give the impression he did not have a care in the world.

The next side street was not as busy. There were not as many lights, either. A rider passed them going in the opposite direction. A woman in a tight dress bestowed a come-hither look from a recessed doorway.

"We should arrest her, too," Toby growled.

"Hell, if it were up to you, half the population would be behind bars," Lester observed. "You have to learn when to bend the law and when not to."

"Don't start on that again," Toby said. "Granted, you

have more experience than me. But I learn fast. And if I'm less willing to turn a blind eye to lawbreakers, it's only because I want to make captain before you."

Lester chuckled. "When I was your age, I was a fountain of vigor and vim, too. But age mellows a man, Tobias. He learns what is important and what isn't. He learns when to get upset and when not to."

"Oh no," Toby said. "Another lecture."

Zach was listening to the tramp of their shoes. Ahead, on the right, the dark mouth of an alley appeared.

"Scoff all you want," Lester chided his partner, "but I've been wearing a badge longer than you have. It wouldn't hurt to listen to me now and then."

"I swear. There are times when you remind me of my father."

Zach glanced over his shoulder. They were so busy bickering they had not noticed the alley. Toby had let the muzzle of the pistol drop, and Lester had not drawn his. Zach casually placed his hand on the hilt of his Bowie, then took it off again. He would not kill them. They were just doing their job.

"What's wrong with that?" Lester was saying. "Josiah is a damn fine man. He asked me to look after you, didn't he?"

"I don't need coddling," Toby spat. "I can take care of myself."

"Never refuse a helping hand, boy," Lester said. "I wish I'd had someone to take me under his wing when I was your age. I might not have made all the mistakes I did."

Zach was abreast of the alley. Spinning, he darted into it, but he went only a few yards. Turning, he crouched and cast about for something he could use as a weapon, but there was only a stack of empty crates against one wall.

"Come back here!" Toby bellowed, and rushed in after him.

Levering upward, Zach punched him where it would

hurt any man the worst. Uttering a strangled gurgle, Toby doubled over, dropping to his knees. Wresting the Hawken from his grasp, Zach pointed it at Lester, who had stopped in the alley mouth and was clawing at his side arm.

"Don't try it," Zach warned.

For a few moments it seemed Lester would draw anyway. His stout body as rigid as a plank, he hesitated.

"Please," Zach said. "I don't want to shoot you, but I will if you make me."

"I wear this badge for a reason."

"And I have a sister to save," Zach said. "She's been kidnapped. They were on the *Astoria*, and when I tried to get to her, the captain sicced his deckhands on me."

Lester's features were hard to read in the dark. "If what you're saying is true, you should go to the law."

"If I do, my sister will be killed." Zach would have said more, but Toby was trying to rise with a pistol in each hand. He slammed the Hawken's stock against the young policeman's temple and, as Toby folded, covered his partner.

Lester had taken a step but stopped. "Hit him again and you'll have to kill the both of us."

"Do you believe me about my sister?" Zach asked.

A long minute elapsed before Lester responded. "My duty is to take you in. Every instinct I have tells me you're telling the truth, though, and I've learned to trust my instincts. They've kept me alive this long."

Toby was still conscious. "No!" he bleated, weakly groping for a weapon. "Shoot the bastard!"

Squatting, Zach reclaimed his flintlocks and tucked them under his wide leather belt. He also relieved Toby of his own pistol and tossed it behind some nearby crates. "What will it be?" he addressed Lester, who had not moved.

The older policeman shifted so his back was to the left wall and held his arms out from his sides. "I hope you find your sister. If you need help, look me up. Lester Hampton. Ask for me at any police station and they'll track me down."

Zach was at the alley mouth. "Thank you," he said. "Tell your partner I'm sorry but I had to do it."

Lester wasn't looking at him. Lester was staring down at Toby, who had risen on his elbows. "Toby, no!" he cried, but it was too late. A clacking sound was wafted on the night wind. It would bring other police who might not be as obliging as Lester Hampton.

Zach ran to the next intersection and went left. At the junction after that, he turned right. People stared, but that couldn't be helped. He had to put as much distance behind him as he could. Intent on watching behind him for pursuit, he had no idea two policemen were in front of him until one shouted.

"Hold it right there! Hands in the air!"

They were fifty feet away, their pistols out and aimed. Zach dug in his heels, jerked his arms aloft, and whipped into the street, past an oncoming carriage. A pistol boomed and a horse whinnied in pain. Running flat out, Zach came to another intersection and turned north.

A hasty glance showed the carriage had stopped and one of the lead horses was down, thrashing in the traces. The driver was railing at the police, but they paid him no mind.

They were after Zach. He was to the end of the next block when the next shot rang out. Angling east, he heard more clacking. Police were converging from all points of the compass and would soon have a net thrown around the area.

Zach had to get out of sight. He would hide until they gave up, then resume his hunt for Evelyn.

A dark structure held promise. It was long and low, and over the front door hung a large sign that read in bold white letters, SMITH BROTHERS, IMPORTS AND EXPORTS

OUR SPECIALTY. He sprinted around the corner and along the building until he came to a window. A sharp push confirmed it was locked. Drawing his Bowie, he was about to try and jimmy the window open when gruff shouts filled the street.

The police were almost on top of him.

Frantic for a spot to hide, Zach raced to the far end of the building. The alley ended at a wall. He had trapped himself. Turning like a wolf at bay, he raised the Hawken.

"Down here! I think he went down here!"

Shadows flitted out near the street.

That was when Zach noticed the building adjacent to Smith Brothers. Windows were spaced every twenty feet or so, and the one nearest to him was ajar. The sill was only eight feet off the ground, so it was the work of an instant for Zach to take a running bound and leap up with his arms outstretched and hook his elbows over the edge. He almost dropped the Hawken. A swift kick and he was inside, rolling on his shoulder. He was in a small, black-as-pitch room. The vague outline of a door beckoned, but Zach turned. Footsteps were pounding down the alley. Quickly closing the window, he locked it and dropped flat.

Someone came to a stop outside. "Do you see him anywhere? I could have sworn I saw him duck in here."

"I don't see anyone," another said. "Damn it, I hope we haven't lost him."

There was a scrape and a thump and a shape appeared at the window. A hand tried to open it. "Locked. I guess I was wrong. We'd better keep looking."

Their footsteps retreated. Zach rose and sprang to the door. The hallway it opened into was narrow and musty. There was no rear exit, so he cautiously padded toward the front.

Zach was even with the next door down when he noticed a thin line of light around the edges. He thought he heard whispering. Anxious to avoid whoever was in there, he crept forward on the balls of his feet.

Suddenly, the door was flung wide open and the muzzle of a pistol was thrust out, inches from his face. "One move and you're dead."

Chapter Eight

What sort of mansion has bars in the windows? That was the
question Evelyn King asked herself as she paced like a rest-
less cougar in the confines of the bedroom where she had
been placed.

Evelyn was scared. More scared than she had been since
she was abducted. She did not like the man Palantine. She
did not like how he looked at her. No one had ever looked
at her the way he did. His glittering eyes devoured her as if
she were a succulent piece of meat.

Then there was all the whispering that went on before
the butler, James, brought her upstairs. Athena and Palantine had been saying things about her, she was sure.
Athena would glance at her every so often and nod, as if
agreeing with whatever their host was suggesting.

As she had twenty times already, Evelyn walked up to
the window and wrapped her hands tight around two of
the bars and strained with all her might. It was pointless.
She was wasting herself. The bars were solid metal. Moving to the door, she put an ear to it but heard nothing. Absolutely nothing at all. The house was as quiet as the deep

woods in the still hour before dawn when the meat-eaters had stopped roaring and snarling and howling and before the creatures that preferred the day came out of their burrows and dens and nests.

Evelyn tried to open it, but the door was the same as it had been the last ten times—locked. She balled a fist and went to punch it but stopped herself. If Athena Borke heard, she would think it amusing, and Evelyn refused to give her captor any measure of pleasure.

She wished she could get her hands on a gun or a knife. Her brother would smile to hear her say that. Zach had always said she was too kindhearted for her own good. He used to tease her that she would make a terrible Shoshone because if her village was ever raided, she would give the raiders milk and cookies instead of counting coup. She always replied that counting coup was for warriors, not women, and he always brought up that when a village was attacked, the women and children were expected to rally to its defense.

"The Shoshone way of life isn't like the white way of life," Zach once said. "All you think of are fancy dresses and a nice house and the theater." He had bobbed his chin at their valley and the craggy snowcapped peaks that ringed it. "The real world is teeth and claws and bullets and blades. The sooner you admit that, the better off you'll be."

Evelyn had been upset with him, as was often the case. So what if the world she liked was not the world he liked. That did not make her world any less desirable. He seemed to blame her for wanting to live where people were not always out to kill one another, and where she could walk out her door without having to worry about running into a grizzly or a mountain lion or a rattlesnake.

In the wilds, that wasn't possible. But in her father's world, the civilized world of cities and towns, where the only animals that roamed free were dogs and cats and poultry and pigs, and killers were thrown into prison and left there until they rotted, a person could live without fear. A person could go her entire life without once being attacked by beasts or men who behaved like beasts.

Is that so bad? Evelyn had often wondered. Her answer was always a rousing, "No!" It was the kind of life she had yearned after for half her young life. To feel safe. To *be* safe.

A knock at the door intruded on her thoughts. The door opened and James stepped inside and bowed. "I beg your pardon, little miss, but my master and Miss Borke want me to escort you to the dining room."

"And if I refuse to go?"

"I am to throw you over my shoulder and carry you. I would rather it not come to that, and I am sure you would, too."

"Did they say what they wanted?" Evelyn asked.

"They did not tell me and I did not ask," James responded. "Mr. Palantine is touchy about his private business. He does not like people to pry. Least of all his servants." James moved aside and beckoned. "After you, little miss."

Her head held high, Evelyn strode out. His hand fell on her shoulder. The hallway curved to a landing, and from there they descended a curved flight of stairs into a grand parlor. James ushered her across it and through a doorway and into a long room that contained a long table and chairs, and little more. The table was of highly polished wood. Mahogany, Evelyn believed it was called. Silverware and glasses had been set out for three people.

At the head of the table sat Palantine, sipping wine from a gold goblet. On his right was Athena Borke. Somewhere or other she had acquired a new black dress with frilly lace at the throat. Over against the wall stood Mateo and Carlos, awaiting her beck and call.

"Miss King!" their host happily exclaimed, and rose out of his chair. "What a delight to see you again. Please, take a seat. My dear friend Athena mentioned she was hungry, and I thought it proper to feed the two of you."

"I don't want any food," Evelyn flatly informed him. It occurred to her that maybe Palantine was unaware of her plight, and she quickly said, "Your dear friend has kidnapped me. What I want is to be let go."

Palantine fixed a stern stare on Athena. "Is this true? Have you taken this fair child against her will?" At that they both laughed heartily.

Evelyn sensed there was more here than met her eyes. "You don't care what she has done?"

"Not one bit, girl," Palantine said. "You see, this isn't the first time. Athena and I share a mutual business interest."

"I don't understand," Evelyn admitted.

"Of course you don't." Palantine reached over and patted the empty chair on his left. "Sit down and all will soon be made clear."

Evelyn would love to turn and bolt, but James was still behind her, his hand on her shoulder. She did as she had been bid and folded her hands in her lap. "Make it clear to me," she said.

Palantine's burning eyes focused on hers. "Before we go any further, let's make one thing clear, shall we? You do not tell me what to do. Ever. I tell you what to do, and when I tell you, you had damn well better do it."

"I don't like you," Evelyn said.

His big hand flicked out and caught her across the cheek with a loud smack. "The second thing for you to remember is to treat me with respect. No sass, ever, or you won't like the consequences."

Shocked, Evelyn touched her cheek and came close to tears. Being struck still shocked her. Neither her father nor her mother ever hit her when she was growing up.

Shoshones did not believe in striking their children; they believed it did more harm than good.

Athena Borke, much to Evelyn's surprise, stiffened and said angrily, "That will be enough of that, Edmund. Need I remind you the girl is under my care?"

Palantine's thick lips quirked. "Grown a conscience, have you? Or is there something special about this one?"

"She is an instrument of revenge, nothing more," Athena said. "But she is *my* instrument, and I will decide how she is to be treated."

Evelyn repressed a shudder when Palantine gave her that hungry look again. She looked at her butter knife but restrained herself.

"So this one is to be spared? What a pity. She's a pretty little snot. And you know how they like the innocent ones."

"I never said she would be spared," Athena responded. "In fact, you've given me an idea I've been mulling over since we arrived."

"I have?" Palantine said, and tearing his gaze from Evelyn, he drained his wineglass. "How so?"

"My current object in life is to make her brother's life as miserable as I can. It was to this end that I kidnapped her." Athena smiled at Evelyn, who stared coldly back. "It has occurred to me that few things would tear him apart more than learning his sister had entered the trade."

"What a marvelous idea!" Palantine exclaimed. "I always have admired your devious bent."

Evelyn did not like the sound of that. "What trade are you talking about?" She imagined being put to work in one of those shops where girls toiled at making garments for twelve hours a day.

"She has no idea, does she?" Palantine said to Athena.

"None whatsoever. She's led a sheltered life up in the mountains. It would never even enter her head."

"What wouldn't?" Evelyn asked.

"Up in the mountains, you say?" Palatine fixed his wolfish gaze on Evelyn once more. "As fresh as a daisy, is that it? Why, I'm tempted to buy her myself. Most of these urchins are not nearly as innocent as they pretend to be."

Evelyn was terribly confused, and admitted, "I don't understand any of this. But whatever you have in mind, I won't go along with it."

"My dear child," Palantine said, "if Athena decides to enter you into the trade, you won't have any choice in the matter. You will be thrown into a locked room and customers will pay quite handsomely for an hour of your time."

"An hour of my—?" Evelyn began, and stopped. Raw horror welled up. "You can't mean—" She could not bring herself to say it.

Athena nodded. "Remember what you saw your mother's brother and his wife doing? There are those who prefer younger companions. Much younger. Even girls your age."

The horror burst full-blown in Evelyn's being and an icy hand enfolded her in its grip. Recoiling, she put a hand to her throat. "You wouldn't!"

Palantine roared with mirth and thumped the table. "I love it when they do that. When it dawns on them, they are completely at our mercy."

Evelyn had to swallow before she could say, "You have done this to others?"

"So many I've lost count," Palantine said. He gestured, encompassing the lavish dining room. "How do you think I can afford all this, girl? I've been in the trade for nigh on twenty years. My clients are some of the most rich and powerful people in the state. Hell, in the country. Athena's husband ran a similar operation in the East, and when he died, she took it over." Palantine winked at Athena. "Quite convenient of him to keel over like that and leave it all to you, eh?"

"All that need concern her is her part in my vendetta against her brother."

"My apologies," Palantine said. "Do you want me to arrange things, then? Or would you rather handle it yourself?"

"We will discuss when and where later. First I must work out how best to use it against her brother."

"That's easy." Palantine held out his glass and James promptly refilled it. "Make the brother watch."

Evelyn thought she would faint. Her brain seemed to go numb and her heart nearly stopped beating.

"Have Zach King watch?" Athena said slowly, her face brightening. "Why, Edmund, you never cease to delight me. That's pure genius."

"I have my moments," Palantine said with false humility. "Plus I've done it a few times myself. Fathers and brothers who entertained heroic notions of saving their daughters and sisters. It tickles me no end when they fall on their knees and beg me to halt the proceedings."

"You're a sadist," Athena said with a grin.

"And damn proud of it, my dear."

Evelyn wanted to shrivel in her chair. She had never met anyone as vile as these two. Never imagined that people could be so wicked, so outright evil. Her mother's people would never do anything like this. The white world, she realized, was not as perfect as she thought it was. "I would die before I let anyone touch me."

Palantine continued to be amused. "They all say that, girl. Well, most, anyway. And do you know what? I've yet to see one take her life. Oh, they bawl and blubber and mope for weeks or months. But eventually they cope.

Granted, they're never the same again. But no one ever said life was a bowl of cherries."

"I hate you," Evelyn declared.

Athena Borke snickered. "You're in good company, Edmund. She hates me, too." Athena toyed with her fork a moment. "About your idea. There's a hitch. Her brother is quite formidable. He's killed Artemis and Phineas, Largo and God knows how many others. Forcing him to watch will take some doing."

"He's only one man," Palantine said, "and I have a small army at my disposal. I'll have him brought alive to wherever you decide to hold the festivities. We'll tie him in a chair and put him in the same room and then stand back and treat ourselves to the spectacle."

"What I wouldn't give to see the look on his face," Athena said.

"Afterward, we can slit their throats and dump them in the river," Palantine proposed. "No one will ever be the wiser."

"Kill Zach King? Spare him years of torment? Not on your life." Athena shook her head. "I intend to destroy him slowly. Starting with his sister here, he will lose everyone and everything he holds dear, just as I lost my brothers."

A man and a woman in crisp white uniforms came through a door at the far end and brought over trays laden with steaming hot food. Palantine and Athena filled their plates to overflowing, but Evelyn refused to help herself to so much as a potato.

"Eat something," Athena Borke commanded. "You must keep your strength up."

"I would rather starve."

"Be stubborn, then," Athena said. "I will simply have you force-fed. It's quite messy and you might choke to death, but you *will* eat, whether you want to or not." She speared a carrot. "The choice is yours."

Clenching her fists, Evelyn bowed her head and closed her eyes. She was so mad, she shook with rage.

"What will it be?" Athena demanded.

Evelyn looked up. "I'll eat." For now she would go along. But she could not take much more of this. Not much at all.

Chapter Nine

Zach King stared into the muzzle of the pistol trained on him and asked, "What's going on?"

The man holding the gun lowered it slightly. He was tall and thin and wore expensive tailored clothes. "I'll ask the questions," he said, nervously glancing up and down the hall. "Who are you? What is all the commotion outside?"

"How would I know," Zach hedged. "Here I am minding my own business and you stick a gun in my face." He looked past the muzzle and past the man and saw a girl seated on the edge of a rumpled bed. She wasn't much older than Evelyn, fifteen or sixteen, maybe, and wore a plain cotton dress and a flower in her hair. Her face had been done up to make her seem older than she was, with red lips and black around the eyes and powder on her cheeks. It only made her look silly, in his estimation.

"I'm sure I heard those infernal nightsticks," the man said. "That means the police are close by." He worriedly licked his lips. "You're certainly not a policeman."

It struck Zach that the man was even more afraid of being caught by the police than he was, and he studied the girl anew, remembering the last female he saw with that much war paint on. "No, I'm not, and I don't care what you're up to." The sounds outside had faded, but he did not want to linger and press his luck.

Suspicion flared in the man's brown eyes. "What exactly are you suggesting?"

"I've had women come up to me on the street," Zach said, and let it go at that. "Now, if you don't mind . . ." He took a step, but stopped when the man thumbed the flintlock's hammer back.

"Not so fast." The man chewed on his lower lip, then motioned for Zach to enter the room. "I swear I will shoot you dead," he vowed when Zach did not comply.

The room was actually a small apartment furnished with a stove and a washbasin. A single lamp afforded pale illumination. The girl sat playing with a strand of her hair and humming to herself.

"I'm sorry," the man said as he closed the door. "But I can't have you going around telling everyone you saw me here."

Zach was near the end of his patience. "What the hell are you talking about? I don't know you from Adam."

"So you claim." The man backed to the bed. "But I can't afford to take the risk. The scandal would ruin me politically." Glancing sharply down at the girl, he snapped, "Stop that infernal humming. I told you before, it bothers me."

"Sorry," she said, and went on doing it.

"Idiot," the man snarled. "I really must talk to him about the quality of the girls of late. It leaves a lot to be desired." He extended the pistol toward Zach. "Turn your back to me. I don't want to shoot you when you're looking at me."

"Are you crazy?" Sometimes it seemed to Zach as if life

had it in for him. "What have I done to deserve being killed?" Too much was happening too fast.

"You're in the wrong place at the wrong time, is all. Now do as I say and turn around."

"If that's what you want. Just don't be hasty," Zach said. Gripping the Hawken by the barrel, he began to turn, then reversed himself, shifting all his weight into the swing. The hardwood stock caught the man across the hand and the flintlock went flying. Howling, the man leaped after it, but Zach was quicker. He clubbed the lunatic on the head and the man folded like a broken doll and lay quivering and mewling.

The girl smiled. "You hurt him. Good. He hurt me."

Zach cautiously opened the door. No one appeared to have heard the commotion. "Close this behind me," he said to the girl, who was rifling the man's pockets. "And stay here until I'm well gone."

Stooped low, Zach padded past more apartments. From a few came muffled sounds, moans and kissing mostly. The hallway ended in a vestibule. Seated in a chair reading a gazette was a greasy character with a potbelly, armed with a brace of pistols and two knives. He turned a page, spied Zach, and came out of the chair as if shot out of it, stabbing a hand to his ample waist.

"Don't," Zach warned, the Hawken leveled.

"Who are you? How did you get in here?"

"All I want is out." Zach wagged the Hawken and the man stepped aside. "A few more steps," he directed, to be safe.

"No one is allowed in here without an appointment." The man blinked. "Charlotte, what are you doing? You're supposed to be with Mr. Linquist."

The girl had followed Zach. She was playing with her hair and had a strand in her mouth and was sucking on it.

In her other hand was a billfold. Only then did Zach notice her eyes were slightly glazed.

"I'm going out, Harry. I need some stuff, and I have the money." Charlotte grinned and wagged the billfold.

"Where did you get that?" Harry demanded. He looked in confusion at Zach, then at her, then at Zach again, and his eyes widened. "So that's it! You're a thief! Working with her!"

I never set eyes on her before today, Zach was about to say, but he only got as far as "I never—" and Harry swooped both hands to his pistols. Zach was not close enough to club him with the Hawken, as he had Linquist. He had no recourse but to shoot.

The impact of the heavy slug lifted Harry off his feet and slammed him against the wall. Like wax oozing from a candle, he melted to the floor, leaving a wide red smear. His mouth moved soundlessly a few times and then he was still.

"You killed Harry," Charlotte said. She did not sound scared or shocked; she was merely stating a fact.

"He didn't leave me any choice," Zach said, and was out the front door as swiftly as his legs could move. The shot was bound to be heard and bring the police. He jumped down a short flight of steps and turned right. At the corner he turned right again. So far no shouts or clacking attended his flight. He sprinted east until a shout brought him to a stop.

"Wait for me! I can't keep up!" The strand of hair was still in Charlotte's mouth, and she was huffing and puffing. "Dang, you're fast, Buckskin. Fast hands. Fast with a gun."

"What do you want?" Zach demanded.

"What kind of silly question is that? We just robbed a man and killed another. We should stick together."

"*You* took that billfold, not me," Zach set her straight. "Go your own way and I'll go mine." He ran on into the night, thinking that was that, but she came after him, struggling to keep up.

"Hold on there, Buckskin! You're making a mistake! I know this city like the back of my hand. Or do you want to spend the rest of your life behind bars?"

Despite himself, Zach slowed and allowed her to pace him. "You're not just saying that? You have lived in New Orleans awhile?"

"All my life." Charlotte spat the strand from her mouth and it hung limp and wet against her pale throat. "The two of us should work together. I can use a partner. Someone handy like you. And you can use someone who knows her way around. What do you say?"

"Get us out of here and we will talk it over" was all Zach would commit to. He had no intention of taking it any further. Once they were in the clear, they would part company so he could get on with his search for Evelyn.

"Stick close, Buckskin," Charlotte said. "You are about to find out why it took Ricard's bullyboys so long to collar me."

Zach had no idea who she was referring to, but he followed her into an alley and along it to a high wall. "What good did this do?" he chafed. It served him right for trusting her. He had trapped himself twice in one night. Tugging at her wrist, he spun. "Why did I believe you? Let's light a shuck."

"Hold on!" Charlotte urged. She pulled him to a corner deep in shadow, dropped onto her knees, and seemed to disappear into the wall itself. "Hurry up, Buckskin!" she urged.

Zach would never have guessed there was a hole large enough for a person to crawl through, but there was. "How did you know about this?" he asked as he stood.

"I told you, silly. I've lived here all my life. On the streets, I mean. You can't help learning stuff."

Charlotte moved with surprising speed. The billfold

had vanished into the folds of her dress, leaving her hands free. Small, delicate hands, as pale as the rest of her.

"Don't you ever get out in the sun?" Zach asked.

The girl broke stride and gave him a peculiar stare. "There's a dumb question if ever I heard one. I work all night and sleep all day. Who cares about the stupid sun, anyway?"

"How old are you?"

"One silly question after another, is that how it's going to be? What difference does it make? But if you must know, in another couple of months I'll be eighteen."

Zach doubted she was a day over fifteen, but he could be wrong. He was not very good at judging how old females were. They hid their age so well.

Another alley brought them to a winding street with more branches than a tree. Charlotte took turn after turn with the purposeful stride of someone as familiar with the city's byways as Zach was with the wilderness he called home. Were it not for the fix he had on the Big Dipper and the North Star, he would be lost.

As Charlotte walked, she prattled. She was one of those who could not keep their mouths shut for more than ten seconds.

"I've been thinking about going off on my own for a long time. I don't like having Ricard and his boys looking over my shoulder. Why, last week I was a couple of dollars short and he beat me like a rug. I can show you the black and blue marks later if you want."

"I'll pass," Zach said, but she did not hear him.

"That's what comes of being forced into the trade. Ricard thinks he owns me. He beats me when he wants, does whatever else when he wants. Just so he always gets his take. Eighty percent of what I make. Can you believe that? Robbery if ever there was any. Doesn't leave much for us working girls, does it? But either we pay up or we have an arm or a leg broken, and that's when he's in a nice mood. When he turns nasty, a girl is likely to turn up as a floater. Not exactly on my list of the ten most wonderful ways to end my life."

Zach was trying to absorb all she said while concentrating on the landmarks. "What is a floater?"

"You don't know?" Charlotte bestowed a look that implied he was half a wagon short of a full load. "A floater is what they call it when they find a body in the river. Ten to fifteen girls in the past year alone. Not that anyone gives a damn. The newspapers always bury it on the back page, and the bodies are planted in potter's field."

"You're saying these girls are murdered?"

"Try to pay attention, Buckskin. I'm explaining all this for your benefit." Charlotte was moving surprisingly fast. Her sluggishness had long since worn off, and her eyes no longer had that glazed look.

"My name is Zach."

"Whatever you say, Buckskin. And yes, girls who skim money or don't do as they're told have a habit of thinking they can breathe water. They're the lucky ones. Those who really get Ricard mad are chopped into bits and fed to gators in the swamps."

"You're serious?" Zach said, and when she nodded, he bounded in front of her and turned. "Hold on a second. If this Ricard does all these terrible things you say he does, why did you steal from that man in the apartment and why are you helping me now?"

"You're awful slow between the ears, Buckskin. I took the money because I need to visit Madame Chou's and that isn't cheap. And I'm helping you because I figure if I do, you'll kill Ricard for me like you killed Harry."

"I'm not an assassin," Zach said coldly.

"You can squeeze the trigger when you have to, and that's what counts. A lot of people don't have the grit."

Charlotte angled past him. Zach frowned and had to move briskly to match her pace. "Listen to me. You're making me out to be something I'm not. I'm grateful for your help, but I'm not about to kill anyone for you."

"Let's talk about this after I'm through at Madame Chou's, shall we?" Charlotte was rubbing her palms back and forth, and the right half of her face twitched as if she were on the verge of a seizure.

"What's the matter with you?"

"Haven't you ever needed something so bad, you couldn't stand it? Something you can't do without no matter how hard you try?"

"I need to find my sister. She's been kidnapped."

Charlotte glanced at him. "No lie?"

Zach told her about Evelyn and the Borkes. A pall of sadness fell over him, and as he finished he averted his face so she would not see his eyes misting over. He missed his sister more at that moment than ever before, and his guilt bubbled to the surface, his shame that he had brought all this on her. It was almost unbearable. So much so, he nearly missed Charlotte's comment.

"I'm sorry about your sis. Maybe I can help you find her."

"What can you do that I couldn't?" Zach said skeptically. He refused to let her raise his hopes.

"I know an awful lot of people, Buckskin, who know an awful lot of people. I can ask around for you. Put out the word. If this Evelyn of yours is anywhere in New Orleans, we'll find her."

Big talk, Zach thought, but that was all it was.

The next street was utterly dark. No streetlights, and all the windows were shuttered. The buildings were occupied, though. Zach heard a baby crying and a woman singing in a language he did not know. Strange scents tingled his nose.

"Here we are," Charlotte announced, bobbing her chin

at a sign written in English: MADAME CHOU'S HOUSE OF ENLIGHTENMENT.

"Enlightenment?" Zach quizzed.

"It's her idea of a joke. She a crusty old gal. I hear they kicked her out of China because she got on the emperor's bad side. Something to do with a nephew of his who died on her premises." Charlotte rapped on the door and a small slot opened. A pair of dark eyes regarded them intently, then a bolt was thrown and light spilled into the street. Charlotte started to go in, then stopped and reached for his hand. "Come on. What are you waiting for? Haven't you ever been in an opium den before?"

Chapter Ten

Evelyn could not say exactly when she made up her mind. It was somewhere between supper and dessert as she listened to Athena Borke and Edmund Palantine openly talk about their foul plans for her and her brother. Of special interest was one exchange.

"Forcing him to watch is all well and good, but finding him poses a problem," Athena said.

Palantine said, "I have hundreds in my employ, my dear, from one end of the city to the other. I will get the word out. Offer, say, a thousand dollars to anyone who can tell me where to find this Zach King. That should do it, don't you think?"

"For that much money, most people would hand him to you on a silver platter," Athena said. "But caution is called for. When you spread the word, be sure to say that under no circumstances must anyone go anywhere near him. He has the instincts of a mountain cat and will sense something is wrong. All they are to do is get word to you and we will take it from there."

"As you wish."

"I mean it, Edmund. You don't know him as I do. He will not let himself be taken alive if he can help it. Discretion is called for. Devious discretion."

Palantine smiled. "At which you are a master. Don't fret. I will do as you want. I will make it clear to my informants that if King suspects he is being watched, I will have the head of the person he suspects. Will that suffice?"

"Quite superbly," Athena said. She dabbed at her mouth with her napkin. "How long do you think it will be before we hear something?"

"There's no predicting, I'm afraid. New Orleans is a big city. It could be hours, it could be days. Why? Are you in a hurry to get somewhere?"

"I was. But it can wait. Tormenting Zachary King takes precedence over everything else." Athena laid the napkin beside her. "I can't tell you how much I appreciate your help. It means a great deal to me. How can I properly thank you?"

Evelyn saw the man called Palantine give Athena Borke that hungry stare of his.

"Forgive my being so frank, but I think you know what that would be. I have made no secret of my desire, and it hurts me deeply that you do not feel the same way."

"I do not give myself to just anyone," Athena said, but a certain warmth had crept into her voice that had not been there before. "I am particular. My standards are not what you would think, and in no way reflect on you personally."

"Small consolation," Palantine said.

Athena threw him a bone. "I will consider it. Most favorably indeed if your plan bears fruit."

"Then you can consider Zach King as good as caught."

As James placed a plate of apple pie in front of her, Evelyn scooped her spoon into it with relish.

"It's nice to see you have come to your senses, child," Athena commented. "Starving yourself would accomplish nothing."

"True," Evelyn agreed. She would not do as well on an empty stomach as she would on a full one. She even went so far as to ask for a second slice, which pleased Borke immensely.

Then came the moment Evelyn was waiting for. Palantine directed James to escort her upstairs.

"Be sure to lock the door behind you. Our young miss is to be our guest for a while yet, and we wouldn't want her getting ideas."

Evelyn already had an idea. She rose when the butler pulled out the chair for her and crossed the dining room with her hands folded in front of her and her head bowed. She wanted them to think her spirit had been broken. That she had given up all hope. It worked, for as she reached the doorway, Athena called out to her.

"Chin up, child. It will all be over soon, one way or the other."

Evelyn looked back and asked a question she had not voiced until now. "What then? What happens to me after you have punished Zach? Will you have me killed?"

"Don't be silly," Athena said, but there was something in the way she said it that made her true intentions plain. "It's your brother I'm after. You are merely a means to an end."

"So you are not going to kill me no matter what?" Evelyn took secret delight in making her say the lie out loud.

"I am not going to kill you. Happy now?"

"Very happy, yes."

Evelyn walked out with her head low and headed down the hall. She could hear James behind her. He did not have his hand on her shoulder as he had when he brought her down. She twisted her head just enough to see him out of the corner of her eye. He was staring at a painting they were passing. It showed a naked and rather plump woman reclining among plush cushions.

There would never be a better moment. Like a doe bolting from a cougar, Evelyn raced down the hallway with her legs flying. Most people would not guess to look at her that she was a mountain girl, born and bred. She had always favored dresses over buckskins, but she had spent as much time outdoors as Zach, doing many of the same things he did: hiking, exploring, climbing trees, playing hide-and-seek and having footraces. Zach nearly always won, but that never stopped her from nearly always accepting his challenge. And she was fast, very fast, faster than many Shoshone girls her age, as she proved by beating them time and again.

Now that fleetness would serve her well. James was big and James was stronger, but James was thick about the middle and not in the best of shape. He yelped and came after her, but she had fifteen feet on him before he lumbered into motion, and when she reached the door at the end of the hall he was thirty feet behind her and rasping like a stricken bull.

Evelyn chose a door on her left at random. She raced down a hall to another that opened into the kitchen. Two men in white aprons were bustling about and did not notice her until she was halfway to yet another door at the other end. An outside door, unless Evelyn missed her guess.

"Stop, missy!" James bellowed.

Evelyn laughed, but it died in her throat as the two kitchen workers moved to cut her off. One was as fat as a bear and pathetically slow, but the other was lean and quick and he almost intercepted her. His outstretched hand missed by inches, and then she was through the door and cool night air fanned her face.

She had done it! Evelyn had to remind herself not to

count her hatchlings before they pecked through the shell. She was outside, yes, but she was still on Palantine's estate. A vast estate, with tilled fields to the east and forest to the northwest. To reach the forest, she had to pass through a back gate in the high wall that enclosed the mansion and the outbuildings. She had no fear of being in the woods at night. After all, she had spent her whole life in them.

The thought jarred her. She used to think of cities as her natural element, as her father might put it. She had always loved the bright lights and the throngs of people and felt more at home in a city than in the high country. Or believed she did. But it wasn't true. Her natural element was the wilderness in which she had been raised. Woodland and wildlife were as much a part of her as the blood in her veins.

The skinny cook was still after her, with James trailing. Evelyn ran as she had not run in years and had twenty-five yards on them when she came to the tree line and plunged in. She looked back. The cook had stopped and was bent over with his hands on his knees, breathless. James was hastening to the mansion for help.

Evelyn would not make it easy for them. The undergrowth was thicker than the undergrowth back home, but she was adept at threading through the worst of tangles. Twice she snagged her dress and once she ripped it, but she did not care. She was free at long last, and that was all that counted.

She was half a mile from the mansion when something snorted in a thicket to her right and the undergrowth crackled to the passage of a large animal. Until that instant, she had not given much thought to what she might run into. There were bound to be cougars and bears. Wild boars, too, she seemed to recollect. Unarmed, she would be helpless should she be attacked. But she could not afford to lose time fashioning a weapon. Not just yet, anyhow.

By now a search party was bound to be after her. Evelyn wondered if Palantine owned dogs. She had not seen any, but on the way out to his estate she had seen a man with a large pack of hounds at the ends of long leashes. Hunting hounds, the kind that could sniff out anything and follow a trail for days.

As if to confirm her worst fear, the night resounded to a wavering bray. It came from the south, from the mansion, and in response half a dozen other hounds raised their canine vocal cords to the stars.

Evelyn broke out in a cold sweat. Eluding people was one thing; eluding the dogs would take a lot of doing. They were swifter than she was, and they need not rely on sight to find her.

She vaulted a log and avoided an oak tree and came on a godsend, a game trail. Newfound confidence filled her, and she flew along it with the grace and speed of an antelope. She must not give in to despair or panic. Hound dogs were expert trackers, but they were, after all, dogs. If nothing else, she should be able to outwit them.

Think, Evelyn! Think! she mentally goaded herself. There had to be a way to throw them off her scent. Climbing a tree wouldn't help. They wouldn't be able to get at her, but they would trail her scent to the bottom of the tree and then stay there braying their fools' lungs out until the search party showed up.

Hard, rocky ground, even if she could find any, would not show prints but would still retain her scent.

No, there was only one way to throw off an animal that relied on its nose. Her father had taught it to her. She needed to find water. There must be creeks in the area. Locating one in the dark would take luck. The vegetation along waterways was often thicker and a shade darker, but in the inky black of night all vegetation looked the same.

Then the trees and the undergrowth thinned and Evelyn's next several steps created small splashes. Hopeful, she came to a stop. But it was not a creek. Before her stretched a swamp, or a bayou, as she believed they were called. Some covered many miles, others a few acres. She could not tell how big this one was. Water was water, though, and the dogs would lose her scent in it.

Evelyn struck off into the swampland. She remembered hearing that swamps were home to snakes, and worse, and she tried not to dwell on that as the water rose to her ankles and then her knees.

Here and there dark islands or hummocks rose from the surface, but Evelyn did not dare set foot on them. It would give her away. She skirted one and heard rustling in the high grass.

The braying of the hounds was far off. Evelyn smiled, thinking of how confused they would be when they reached the swamp and could not smell her anymore. She took another step and felt something brush her left shin. Something soft and slithery. It sent goose bumps erupting up her spine and she halted, half terrified it was a water moccasin or some other venomous serpent. Seconds went by and nothing else happened. Steeling herself, she pressed forward.

Evelyn was all too aware of the risk she was taking. It was exactly the sort of thing she had long despised. Life in the mountains was a never-ending parade of perils. She had been stalked by mountain lions, charged by grizzlies, set on by hostile Indians, and those were just a few. It got so she hated it. She hated having to always be on her guard. She hated never being able to completely relax when she was outdoors.

Was it any wonder, then, Evelyn asked herself, that she

had looked so fondly on the white world? Somehow she had gotten it into her head that the white world was different. That there were no perils to face. That people could live their entire lives without ever having to worry that something would try to eat them or someone would try to kill them.

She had been wrong. She saw that now. Like the surface of this swamp, the surface of the white world was deceiving. On the surface all seemed peaceful and good, but under the surface lurked all kinds of vicious things. Snakes like the one that had brushed her leg, only they walked on two legs. And where a normal snake might lash out to defend itself, the two-legged kind hurt others because they liked it.

Indians hurt people, too, but not in the way those like Athena Borke and Edmund Palantine did. Indians went on the warpath and counted coup, and some tribes were known to torture captives. But they did not force young girls to offer their bodies for money. They did not spread deceit and death as if it were a plague.

Evelyn had a lot to ponder when she got back home. The white world looked much different to her now than it had a few months ago. It was not like the fairy tales her father read to her when she was small. The fancy ladies in their fine clothes and grand homes were like pretty ribbons sprinkled on quicksand.

A sound to her rear startled her. Freezing, Evelyn glanced back. It came from the woods bordering the swamp, but what it had been she could not say. The dogs were still far off, but maybe some of her pursuers were ahead of the pack, although how anyone could have followed her in the dark, she could not say.

When the sound was not repeated, Evelyn continued deeper into the swamp. She was not one to spook easy, but she could not shake a sense that she might have made a mistake. A swamp was no place to be in broad daylight. At night it was vastly worse. But she could not turn back if she wanted to. The notion of falling into Athena Borke's clutches again would not let her.

Another hummock loomed, higher than the rest. Evelyn was dearly tempted to climb out and rest. Small trees dotted it, and there was a log near the water's edge. But she shook her head and went to go around.

The log moved. Part of it came off the ground and swung in her direction, and it voiced a grunt of surprise or warning.

Terror spiked through Evelyn and rooted her where she stood. Swamps harbored many other animals besides snakes. One, in particular, was as fearsome as any creature alive. As savage as a rabid wolf, as tough to kill as a grizzly, it was the lord of its domain. Grown men armed with rifles were loath to tangle with the larger ones because they knew their bullets would not stop it. Unarmed little girls stood no chance at all.

The alligator slid down the bank into the water, but it did not submerge. Its snout and head and part of its tail showing, it swam slowly toward her, its eyes gleaming in the starlight.

Evelyn was too petrified to move, to speak, to do anything other than await the inevitable. She thought of her mother and father and Zach, and how they would never know what happened to her, and how unfair it all was.

Then the alligator opened its mouth.

Chapter Eleven

The first thing Zach King noticed was the smoke that hung in the air, smoke so thick he swore he could cut it with his Bowie. The second thing was the smell, somewhat like that of roasting acorns. The place was cramped and dark. He knew little about opium dens other than that they existed, and that his father once said he should avoid them as he would a grizzly's lair.

The man who admitted them was Chinese. He wore a small circular cap and baggy clothes. Smiling and bowing, he held his hand out to Zach and said in a lilting accent, "Guns and knife, if you please."

Zach took a step back. "Not on your life." He would be damned if he would hand them over with the entire New Orleans police force out after him.

"Don't be a lunkhead," Charlotte said. "Weapons aren't allowed. You'll get them back when we leave." She pointed at a nook lined with shelves filled with pistols and knives and daggers. Propped in the corners were several rifles and swords.

"I don't like this," Zach said.

"Do you want my help or not?" Charlotte retorted. "After I'm done here, we'll start looking for your sister." Her face was twitching and she was impatiently tapping her foot. "Come on, Buckskin. I need it. I really need it."

Zach did not ask what "it" was. But he did as she wanted and handed the Hawken and his two flintlock pistols and the Bowie to the smiling doorman, who bowed again and carried them to the nook and carefully set the pistols and the knife on a shelf and leaned the Hawken in a corner.

"There. Satisfied?" Charlotte said, and took his hand.

Zach almost pulled loose. He did not like her touching him. He did not like to be touched, period, unless it was by one of the few people in the world he cared for.

"Where is she?" Charlotte anxiously asked, tapping her foot harder than ever.

"Who?"

Zach's answer came in the form of a stately older Chinese woman in a long dress who materialized out of the shadows. She had her forearms up her sleeves and walked with an odd shuffling gait, taking much smaller steps than it seemed she needed to. Smiling demurely, she bowed. "Young Charlotte. What a pleasure to have you visit my humble establishment again." Her English was impeccable.

"You have the best den in the city, Madame Chou," Charlotte complimented her. "No one is ever robbed, no one is ever molested, and you don't stint with the opium."

"I take great pride in what I do," Madame Chou said. "And in always giving my customers the best their money can buy." Her hooded eyes narrowed. "Which reminds me, young Charlotte. The last time you were here there was a question of payment, if you will recall?"

Seemingly from out of the smoky air, Charlotte produced the billfold with a flourish and counted out several bills. "This should more than cover how much I was short last time, and I have plenty more where that came from."

She opened the billfold wide so Madame Chou could see the rest of the money.

"My, oh my. You have struck it rich, young Charlotte."

"I wish. But this will do for now."

Madame Chou clapped her hands and a Chinese girl not much older than Charlotte came from another nook. "May Ling will see that you are settled in." She switched her attention to Zach. "What about your handsome friend?"

"I'm not here to smoke opium," Zach set her straight.

"Indeed?" Madame Chou frowned at Charlotte. "You know the rules. If he does not smoke, he must leave."

"Can't you make an exception? He and I have things to talk about." To sweeten her appeal, Charlotte held out twenty dollars.

The rapidity with which it vanished up Madame Chou's sleeve was remarkable. "I have been known to bend the rules on occasion. May Ling, show our two fine guests to their space."

A curtain parted, and they were led into a winding labyrinth of shadowed passageways and cubbyholes. To Zach it was a bewildering maze he doubted he could unravel on his own. Again and again he had to duck under low beams. All the cubicles were occupied, many by Chinese but just as many by those who weren't. All the occupants were either puffing on a pipe or lying in a dreamy state of bliss on a bunk or a cot or a pile of blankets.

Zach had never seen the like. Never conceived that people would do this to themselves. He did not see the point. To him, they were the same as those who spent their lives with their mouths glued to a whiskey bottle, and he hated whiskey almost as much as he hated people who hated half-breeds. He had seen what whiskey did. Seen how it turned warriors into weaklings, how it broke strong men on the rocks of unquenchable need. He would never let that happen to him.

At last May Ling stopped beside a curtain and opened it. "I will return with your pipe shortly."

Charlotte eagerly hopped onto a small bunk and rubbed her hands in expectant glee. "It's been a week and a half. I can't wait."

"Why do you do this to yourself?" Zach wanted to know.

"It makes me feel good," Charlotte said. "For a while I can forget all my troubles and woes. I can forget I'm all alone in the world. Forget I make my living by letting pigs paw me. Forget how rotten life is, and how I wish I were dead."

"You need not live like you do. You are young. You are pretty. You can do anything you put your mind to."

Charlotte tilted her head and bored her eyes into his, then sighed. "You honestly believe that, don't you, Buckskin? That the world is a wonderful place and we can all be happy if we will only put our minds to it?"

"I never said that," Zach said stiffly.

"It's a silly notion. I don't know where you're been keeping yourself all your life, but in the real world, the world I live in, life is a struggle to stay alive. No one cares about anyone else. It's every person for themselves."

"Your parents cared for you, I would wager."

"Don't talk about things you know nothing about. You would lose the bet. To them I was a nuisance. The night they dropped me off at the orphanage was the happiest of their lives."

Zach sank cross-legged onto a cushion. "You're just saying that because what they did makes you mad."

"I'm saying it because it's true. I was an accident they didn't want. They put up with me until I was eight, and then one rainy night they bundled me in a blanket and left me on the orphanage doorstep." Charlotte paused. "I will never forget how they were smiling and laughing and holding hands as they walked off."

Without thinking, Zach said, "My parents would never do that to me."

"Rub it in, why don't you? Just don't sit there and tell me the world is all sugar and cream when I know better. The world is a dagger waiting to stab you in the back. Not once, but every day of your life."

Zach could not come up with anything to say that would change her mind other than "There's more good in the world than you'll admit. One day you're bound to meet someone special and fall in love, and you'll see I'm right."

Charlotte laughed teasingly. "Why, Buckskin. I would never have taken you for the romantic kind. Love solves all our woes? Is that how it goes?"

Zach's reply was forestalled by the arrival of May Ling with the items Charlotte would need on a long tray. Charlotte eagerly reached up for it and set it down in front of her. May Ling bowed and left them.

On the tray sat a lamp and a box carved from the horn or antler of an animal. Exactly what kind of animal was impossible for Zach to tell. The box was filled with a black paste so thin it was almost liquid. Also on the tray were a wire, a small stone bowl, and a thin length of bamboo.

Zach watched as Charlotte picked up the bowl and screwed it onto the bamboo stem. She then used the wire to dip out some of the paste and held it to the lamp's flame. The heat hardened the paste, and when its consistency suited her, she pressed it into the bowl and commenced inhaling through the bamboo, drawing the smoke deep into her lungs.

Closing her eyes, Charlotte moaned and asked, "Are you sure you don't want some, Buckskin? There's nothing like it in all the world."

"No, thanks," Zach answered. He found it mildly disgusting.

The ball of paste did not last long. Charlotte immediately prepared another. And a third. Smoke trickled from her nostrils with every breath she took. "You have no idea what you are missing."

Zach had a more important concern. "How long before we start asking around about my sister?"

"Just be patient," Charlotte said. "We can't do much before daylight, so you might as well relax and enjoy yourself."

Frustrated, Zach sat back and glowered. She was too preoccupied to notice. Her movements became slower and slower until her arms hung limp at her sides and her head lolled back. Her face had grown severely pale, and her eyes were glazed and empty. "Charlotte?" he said, but she did not answer.

"Wonderful," Zach said. Folding his arms across his chest, he considered whether to leave her there and search alone. He almost did. He coiled his legs under him to rise, but the sight of her sitting there so lifeless and helpless deterred him.

Curious, Zach picked up the pipe and sniffed the bowl. He sniffed the contents of the box, too. Feeling slightly light-headed, Zach swished at the smoke. Directly across from their cubicle was another. All the bunks were occupied by Chinese opium addicts. Most were in the same shape as Charlotte. One was puffing on a pipe, his slitted eyes fixed on Zach in what Zach construed as a mocking smirk.

"What are you looking at?" Zach demanded, but he might as well have asked the walls.

"This was a mistake," Zach said to Charlotte, whose expression now was one of total and utter bliss. Sighing, he sat back and leaned his head on the cushion and closed his eyes. He had not slept in two days and he was bone tired. A short rest would do him some good.

His fatigue took its toll. Zach was not aware of drifting off. He had slept he knew not how long when he sensed movement nearby and struggled up out of a dreamless fog to find May Ling on her knees beside him, about to touch his face. Startled, he sat up, and equally startled, she drew back and put her hand to her throat.

"What are you up to?" Zach demanded.

"I am most sorry," the Chinese girl said, bowing her forehead low to the floor. "I thought you were in the opium world like your friend."

"I like this world just fine, thanks," Zach said. Suspicion pricked at him, and as she started to slide back, he snapped, "What were you after? Trying to take my poke while I was out, is that it?"

"Oh, no, sir," May Ling said most earnestly. "I would never rob you or anyone else. Madame Chou would have me sent back to China. She runs a respectable establishment."

"So she claimed." Zach wasn't entirely convinced. "But if it wasn't that, then what?"

May Ling shifted in embarrassment. "Please, sir. It was nothing. Permit me to leave you in peace."

"Not until you fess up."

"Fess up?" May Ling said. "Oh. You want me to tell you?" She looked at him imploringly, and when he did not relent, she said contritely, "I only wanted to touch you, nothing more."

"Why on earth would you want to do that?" Zach's suspicions mounted. She *had* tried to rob him and was concocting an excuse.

"You will think it silly of me."

"Try me," Zach said. Silly or not, he should drag her to Madame Chou and raise a little hell.

May Ling looked at the floor, not at him. "Many people

come here. Many Chinese. Many Americans. Some Creoles. Some Spanish. Some French. But never someone like you before."

"Like me?"

"An Indian." May Ling glanced up. "You are an Indian, are you not? You look like the few I have seen. Your hair. Your face."

"I'm half-and-half," Zach said. "A mongrel, you might say." He could have added that both his father's and his mother's people tended to look down their noses at him, but he didn't.

"Only half Indian?" May Ling sounded disappointed. "I am twice as sorry for needlessly disturbing you."

"Even if I were a full-blooded Shoshone, what purpose did touching me serve?"

"I wanted to feel how your skin feels. I wanted to run my fingers through your hair. Last week, a loud Russian came in. His skin was rough and pink, his beard coarse. Before him there was a man from Sweden with hair as fine as silk that shone in the light like gold."

"It still makes no sense," Zach said. "You touch folks just to touch them?"

"Do you not do the same when you come across something new? Do you not like to examine it?"

Zach glanced at the opium pipe and the box with the black paste. "Sure. Most everyone does. But no one does it with people." Preposterous as it seemed, he believed she was telling the truth.

"My mother has always said I am too curious," May Ling said. "You will not tell Madame Chou, will you? She does not like to have her guests disturbed."

"My lips are sealed," Zach said, and received a grateful look as the Chinese girl hurried down the shadowy passageway. Shaking his head, he made himself comfortable and lay there for the longest while thinking about Athena

Borke and the hundred and one ways he could deprive her of her life.

Sleep claimed him. He had the most fantastic dreams. One was of his childhood, of his mother and father and Evelyn and him seated around the table, eating and laughing. Those were wonderful times.

When he finally woke up, Zach was slow to stir. Arching his back, he stretched to relieve a cramp. It was a few seconds before he realized Charlotte was gone.

Chapter Twelve

When Evelyn King was six, her father and mother sat her down one day to impart important advice. They explained to her how much they liked living in the Rocky Mountains. Her father liked the freedom most, how he could do whatever he wanted whenever he wanted with no one looking over his shoulder telling him how it should be done. Her mother liked the beautiful valley in which they lived. She liked the pretty wildflowers and the butterflies and the emerald lake and the ivory-capped peaks.

Evelyn had told them that she liked it there, too. She liked the squirrels that chattered at her from the tall pines, and the does and their fawns that would graze near the lake at dawn and dusk. She liked how the chipmunks were always scampering madly about and would chitter angrily at anything and everything.

Yes, they lived in a paradise, her father called it. But paradise had a dark side. A dangerous side. Not all animals were as adorable as the chipmunks. Some animals would kill them if they could. Just as they ate venison and elk meat, there were animals that would eat them.

"I do my best to keep the meat-eaters out of our valley," her father had said. "But I can't be everywhere at once, and it's a big valley. You must always keep watch for things that might harm you."

It was a long list of things. Bobcats, when she was little, might think she was small enough to bring down. Coyotes, if they were hungry enough and she was off in the woods alone, might decide she was edible. Wolves, in the cold of winter when the packs were starving, would not hesitate to kill her. Black bears, which were unpredictable and might as soon run as attack her. Mountain lions, which nearly always attacked from behind or above and would give her no warning whatsoever. And the most fearsome of all, the animal all others were afraid of, a beast that could crush her with one swipe of a giant paw or one snap of its iron jaws: the mighty grizzly.

Their talk made a deep impression. Evelyn had never seen her mother and father so serious, never heard such worry in their voices and seen such worry in their eyes. They were genuinely scared for her, and she became scared for herself.

From that day on, Evelyn changed. She did not love their valley as much as she had before. It had become a terrible place, a frightening place. For every sunlit glade there were patches of shadow that might hide a lurking predator. Her parents never let her wander into the woods unarmed, and that in itself was depressing. She always had to wear the small pistol her father bought in St. Louis just for her, or tote the small Hawken rifle he had custom-made for her. They were constant reminders that the next crack of a twig she heard might be her last.

It got to the point where Evelyn hated it. She hated always having to look over her shoulder. She hated living on the raw edge of life day after day after day. In some ways, she felt like those does and their fawns. The deer, too, must always stay alert, must never relax their vigilance, or they, too, would wind up as something's food.

To reduce the odds of that happening, her father and mother gave her tips on how to spare her hide from the teeth and claws of the animals that would want to rip and rend it. She was to never go far from the cabin alone. She must always tell one or the other where she was going and how long she thought she would be gone. She must stop often to look and listen, and just as often look behind her.

The key to staying alive, as her father put it, was to spot a meat-eater before it spotted her. But should the unthinkable occur, should she be confronted by a creature that saw no difference between her flesh and deer flesh, she must never, ever run from it. Fleeing, her parents said, would only cause the mountain lion or grizzly to come after her. She stood a better chance if she stared them down.

"Can't I just back away nice and slow?" Evelyn had asked.

"Sometimes that works, sometimes not," her father had replied. "No two animals react the same."

"Standing still is best," her mother insisted, "especially when they are so close to you that you can reach out and touch them."

Now, alone in the bayou, standing so close to an alligator that she could reach out and touch its snout, Evelyn remembered that day long ago and the advice her parents gave her. She stood stock-still, meeting the gator's gaze with her own and hoping to heaven it could not smell the fear that filled her.

The alligator closed his jaws with a loud snap. Why it had opened and closed its mouth like that was a mystery, but at least it had not sunk its razor teeth into her.

Cold sweat caked Evelyn. She fought down a shiver and stood her ground, waiting for the gator to make up its mind. Evelyn thought of her brother and of her mother and father, and the sadness that these days never left her heart seemed to spread throughout her whole body so that it was all she could do not to cry.

A minute went by, and all the gator did was stare. Evelyn wondered if it was waiting for her to break and run. It would be on her before she took two steps. It would seize her and go under and roll over and over until she stopped struggling, then either devour her or cache her to eat later.

Evelyn could not stand there forever. Her nerves could not take the strain. Suddenly flapping her arms, she shouted, "Go away! Leave me alone!"

The alligator did nothing. Absolutely nothing at all.

Emboldened, Evelyn backed up a step, and then another. The gator did not move. She kept going, moving her legs slowly so as not to splash and placing each foot down with extreme care. Six feet separated them. Then eight feet. Then twelve. She was beginning to believe she had been worried for no reason when the alligator exploded into motion and hurtled toward her like a living battering ram.

Evelyn did what most anyone would have done. She screamed and whirled and ran. Her legs impeded by her soaked dress, she could not move fast enough. Not anywhere near fast enough.

Water rippling in its wake, the alligator closed with frightening speed. There was no mistaking its intent.

Evelyn turned at bay and cast frantically about for a weapon—a branch or a stick with which she could gouge at its eyes and maybe drive it off. But there was only the water, soon to be her grave.

Suddenly, from out of the night behind her, shadows glided past on either side. One instant they were not there, the next they were, placing themselves between her and the gator.

Evelyn was too stupefied to speak. It seemed unreal,

their being there, but they were, as dark and sinister and nearly identical as always, each with a long blade held low.

"Stay where you are, little one," Mateo said. The scar on his chin was hard to see in the dark.

"Our mistress wants you alive," Carlos said, "and that is how we will take you to her."

The alligator, Evelyn saw, had stopped.

"You or I, brother?" Carlos asked.

"Me," Mateo answered, and began circling slowly to the right, his knife held so the cutting edge was on top. He never took his eyes off the alligator, and the alligator never took its eyes off of him. It turned as he did, keeping him always in front.

"When we move," Carlos said out of the corner of his mouth to Evelyn, "you must run. Just in case it gets past us. Run until you reach solid ground and stay there. The dogs and the others will be here soon enough."

"What do you mean by 'move'?" Evelyn asked, but he was focused on the alligator and only the alligator, his whipcord body coiling like a spring. It dawned on her that they were going to attack it. Sheer folly, she thought, for no man, no two men, were a match for an alligator in its own element. But then she remembered that some people had said the same thing about grizzlies, yet her father was known as Grizzly Killer, the man who had slain more of the great bears than anyone else.

Mateo was still slowly circling. The alligator was still turning with him. Its right side was toward Carlos, not its maw or its powerful sawtooth tail, and that must have been what the brothers had intended all along, because suddenly Mateo cried out and lunged, thrusting at the gator's head. But it was only a feint, a trick to distract the alligator for the few heartbeats it took Carlos to spring in next to the reptile and shear his long knife up into its unprotected belly.

The alligator whipped around, but Carlos had already sliced it open and was backpedaling out of its reach. The gator started to come after him, and in so doing, exposed the underside of its neck to Mateo. Again cold steel flashed, and again a spreading stain tinted the water even darker.

Evelyn could not help but be impressed. The twins had fought as if they were one instead of two. Each seemed to know what the other would do before the other did it. Each was deadly in his own right; together, they were as lethal as the most lethal carnivore in all of Louisiana.

For by now the alligator was thrashing the water in its death throes. Mateo skipped back as its trail churned the water to a froth. Then, as calmly as if he were strolling along a city street, he wiped his knife clean on his pants, sheathed it, and casually strolled to his brother's side.

"This one was slow."

"Or perhaps we only thought they were faster when we were young," Carlos said. "It is not as much fun as it used to be." They turned, and Carlos said, "I thought I told you to run."

Evelyn watched the alligator sink beneath the surface upside down. A flurry of bubbles marked the spot where it breathed its last. "You killed gators when you were boys?"

"We grew up near a swamp," Mateo revealed. "Our father was a sharecropper, and we were always poor. To eat, we had to keep food on the table. We killed gators, and everything else that crawled, walked, swam, or flew."

"Those were great days," Carlos said fondly.

Evelyn gazed at each in turn. "And now you kill people for Athena Borke."

"Our mistress, as she likes us to call her, is most generous," Mateo said. "She pays us well for our services. Far better than anyone else ever has."

"You'll kill my brother if you have the chance, won't you?"

"We already had the opportunity," Carlos answered. "At the gangplank on the *Astoria*. But we let him live. It is our mistress's wish he not be harmed until she decides the time is right."

"If I had pistols, I would shoot you both," Evelyn told them.

The twins each took her by an arm and headed her toward shore. "We believe you would, little one," Mateo said. "That is why we respect you."

"Sure you do."

"I never lie," Mateo said. "Most girls your age would have broke by now. They would weep and moan and beg and be terrified of our mistress and of us. They would never think to kill us, because they have never killed a soul. You could do it. We see it in your face. And we respect you for that."

"I don't want your respect," Evelyn declared, but in a strange sort of way, she was highly flattered.

Carlos was sheathing his knife. "You misjudge us, child. When we kill, it is never personal, just our job."

"If you're telling the truth," Evelyn clutched at a straw, "prove it. Let me go. No one will ever know you found me."

"Do us the courtesy of treating us with the same respect we treat you," Mateo said. "What kind of men would we be if we lied to our mistress and did not do as she commanded us?"

"We are not without honor," Carlos remarked. "In that regard, we are no different from your brother."

"What do you know about Zach?" Evelyn baited him.

"He killed Artemis Borke to uphold the honor of his people," Carlos said. "He killed Phineas Borke to uphold the honor of his family. We would have done the same were we in his place."

"Then how can you kill him if Athena tells you to?"

"Because *our* honor requires it," Mateo said. "We have pledged our loyalty to her, before all else and all others."

Evelyn's legs were cold from her knees down, and her feet were coated with muck. "All I know is that I would never want anything to do with a woman who has no honor, and I am surprised you do."

The twins glanced sharply at her, and Carlos said sternly, "That will be enough, little one. We respect you, yes. But we will not be insulted."

They did not speak after that until they came to the pack and the handlers, and figures on horseback.

Athena Borke dismounted and walked up to Evelyn and flicked a fingernail across her chin. "You gave us quite a chase, my dear. I should whip you within an inch of your life, but you would fetch a lower price."

"Don't touch me," Evelyn said.

Palantine had a cape over his shoulders and a sword at his hip, and he sat his horse as one who was not comfortable in the saddle. "If you ask me, Athena, you are too lenient with the brat. Give her to me for an hour, and when I am done she will never talk back to you again."

"You were never one for subtlety, Edmund."

They had brought a spare horse. Mateo boosted Evelyn into the saddle. Then he and his brother mounted and hemmed her between them.

"So you don't get any more foolish ideas into that silly head of yours," Athena said. "Now let's get back. You need to rest so you will be bright and fresh for the auction tomorrow."

"Auction?" Evelyn said.

"Why, yes, child. It's Edmund's idea. We are inviting some of the richest people in New Orleans to bid for the right to do with you as they please. Once we have your brother, of course. I want him to have a front-row seat, as it were."

"Zach is too smart for you. You won't catch him," Evelyn declared.

Athena Borke laughed.

Chapter Thirteen

The warren of dark passageways was as confusing as ever. Zach King had been wandering them for what must have been a quarter of an hour, fruitlessly seeking Charlotte, when he rounded a corner and nearly collided with May Ling, who had her back to him. "Where is she?" he demanded. "Where did she get to?"

May Ling's long dress rustled as she turned. She had her small hands folded in front of her. "Do you mean your friend, young Charlotte? She left an hour ago."

"But she said she would help—" Zach began to blurt, and stopped himself. He had been a fool to think he could rely on her.

"Very few are still here," May Ling mentioned.

Zach had seen that for himself. Scarcely six occupied bunks in the whole place. "I would like to leave, too." He could not bring himself to admit he could not find his way out, but she understood.

"Follow me, please."

"Have you ever heard of a woman named Athena Borke?" Zach asked as they navigated the twisting turns and bends. Since he couldn't count on Charlotte, he would find Borke himself.

"The name is not familiar," May Ling said. "But many who come here do not use their real names."

"Why not?" Zach had, when Charlotte introduced him.

"Madame Chou's establishment, and the many others like it in the city, are not viewed with favor by some high in authority. They want to close such establishments and deport all Celestials."

Zach vaguely remembered that some people referred to the Chinese in that manner. After what he had seen, he was inclined to agree with those who thought opium dens were a vice, not a virtue, but he did not say so.

"I confess I do not understand why," May Ling went on. "Those who indulge in our services are never violent or quarrelsome like those who drink too much at taverns and saloons. Opium quiets the passions. It does not excite them."

She had a point there, Zach conceded, but lying on a bunk for hours staring endlessly off into space like a human vegetable did not strike him as natural. "Do you smoke opium yourself?"

"Oh, never. Madame Chou does not allow it."

The same Chinese man was on duty. He cheerfully returned Zach's weapons, bowing as he did so. Zach was wedging his pistols under his belt when someone rapped on the door in the same series of knocks Charlotte had used. The man quickly opened the small slot, closed it, and opened the door.

Daylight spilled inside, the sun so brilliant, Zach squinted against the glare. A black man in a costly suit and polished boots came in and removed his high hat.

A free black, Zach figured, not one of the many slaves that made up a large percent of the city's population. Slaves could not afford such fine clothes.

"Is Madame Chou here?" the black asked May Ling. "I have a message for her."

"I am sorry, Mr. Frayne. She retired a while ago."

"It's important," Frayne said. "I was roused out of bed at four this morning and instructed to visit all the dens on this side of the city and speak to the proprietors in person so they can spread word to their customers." He had not paid much attention to Zach, but he did so now, and blinked a few times. Then, smiling broadly, he said, "We don't often see frontiersmen in a place like this. Whom do I have the honor of addressing?"

Zach told him.

"Jack Frayne, at your service," the black man said in the typical courtly fashion of a New Orleans gentleman.

"And what do you do, Mr. Frayne?" Zach idly asked, sheathing his Bowie.

"I work for one of the richest men in the city," Frayne divulged. "I and several associates are what you might call his lieutenants."

It occurred to Zach that Athena Borke was ungodly rich, as well, and that rich people tended to travel in the same social circles. "Have you by any chance ever met a woman named Athena Borke?"

Frayne pursed his lips. "No, I can't say as I have. Is she a friend of yours, Mr. King? If I am not being too personal."

"Someone I must find," Zach said, and got out of there. He had to shield his eyes with a hand until they adjusted to the bright morning sun. At the end of the street, he paused, debating what to do. He was upset with himself for sleeping the night away. He remembered the glimpse he had of Evelyn on the *Astoria*, and was flooded with fresh guilt.

The day had barely begun and the narrow streets were largely deserted. Zach went in the general direction of the waterfront. Athena Borke had tried to escape by boat once. She might try again. He would find a list of departures and visit every ship leaving for New York City.

Zach had gone only a few blocks when feet pattered behind him and the last person he expected hollered, "Hey! Wait up!"

Charlotte was out of breath from running, and she was angry. "Why did you go off and leave me like that? I thought we were partners? You're lucky I found you."

"May Ling told me you had left."

"I was with Madame Chou. She told May Ling we weren't to be disturbed for any reason."

"So May Ling lied?" Zach said in disgust. She had seemed so nice, so sincere. If nothing else, it was a reminder never to trust a city dweller, white or any other hue, as far as he could throw them.

"She was only doing what was expected of her. But that's neither here nor there." Charlotte yawned and scratched herself and announced, "I'm hungry enough to eat a cow. What do you say we have our breakfast, then go find that sister of yours?"

"I am not hungry," Zach said.

"Well, I am, and I think you are too, but you're too mulish to admit it." Charlotte hooked her warm arm through his. "We'll do better on a full stomach than an empty one. And I know a place not far from here that serves delicious breakfasts. Come on."

Zach let her lead the way. She was bubbling with vitality, a far cry from the sluggish sloth of the night before. "You are different today."

"I'm always starved and raring to go after a night at a den." Charlotte smoothed her plain dress and adjusted the flower in her hair. "How do I look, handsome?"

"Fine," Zach said. In truth, she was quite pretty, but he did not dwell on that. He thought of his wife instead.

"Don't you worry, Buckskin. We'll find your sister.

Someone is sure to have heard of that Borke woman. After we eat, we'll ask around at all the best hotels. A woman like her wouldn't stay in just any old dump."

"I have already asked around at them," Zach said. It was one of the first things he did on reaching the city.

"No offense, but I might be able to loosen lips you couldn't. That scowl of yours would scare most people into clamming up."

The restaurant was dingy and dusty and packed. Charlotte squeezed into a corner booth and patted the seat beside her. "Plant yourself, Buckskin."

Zach would rather not sit so close to her, but all the other seats were taken. When the harried waitress finally came to take their order, he said, "I'll have coffee and toast."

"You call that a meal?" Charlotte scoffed. "He'll have three eggs and ham and potatoes, and I'll have the same."

"You take many liberties," Zach observed after the waitress left.

"Do I? Well, one of us has to or you would starve yourself to death." She patted his hand. "You need to learn to relax more. To enjoy life."

"You wouldn't say that if it was your sister who was missing."

"I'm sorry, Buckskin. I keep forgetting she's all you can think about. I don't blame you, though. You love her, and that says a lot about your character." Charlotte had not taken her hand off his, and now she gave a little squeeze. "I wish I had someone who cared for me as much as you do for Evelyn."

"She's my sister. Why wouldn't I?"

"Hell, Buckskin. I've known a lot of brothers and sisters who hated each other's guts. I always thought they were stupid. I mean, here I am, with no family at all. I'd give anything to have a relative. Brother, sister, cousin, aunt, I wouldn't care."

"You don't know where any of your relatives are?" Zach asked.

"Not a one. I can't rightly go back to the orphanage to check their records after I ran off on them. They would throw me in a room and throw away the key. They never did like me much. Claimed I was too troublesome."

"I could go to the orphanage and check for you," Zach offered, and quickly qualified it by adding, "After we find Evelyn, that is."

Charlotte's face grew soft and rosy. "You would do that for me? Honest to God?"

"Why not? You are helping me. It is only fair."

"Well, now," Charlotte said softly, and looked down at her lap. "They have any more like you back in the mountains? Someone who isn't married, maybe?"

Zach thought of his neighbors, if they could be called that. Five families stretched over a hundred miles, each isolated from the rest of the world by high peaks and endless plains. "All the ones I know are married. The white ones, anyway."

Charlotte let go of his hand and grinned. "I doubt I'd make a good Indian. I hear they live in houses made of stinky buffalo hides and are filthy with fleas and lice."

Someday Zach would like to meet whoever had come up with that falsehood. She wasn't the first one to mention it. "Their houses are called lodges and they are as clean as any white house. And Indians wash and comb their hair just like white people." He did not tell her that some used a mix of bear fat and urine to make their hair shiny.

"Don't get touchy on me," Charlotte said. "I was repeating what folks say. I have nothing against Indians. If I did, I wouldn't be helping you."

They talked about the Shoshones. She asked a hundred and one questions, each answer provoking a new one. He was grateful when their food arrived, and amazed at how she tore into hers like a starving wolf into an elk. She finished before he did, and he was hurrying so they could get out of there that much sooner.

"Now we're ready to pound the streets," Charlotte said, contentedly rubbing her belly.

She paid and they stepped out into the midmorning glare. Conscious that the police were probably still after him, Zach glanced both ways and saw someone at the far end of the street, peering at them from around a corner. He had a definite impression of a black face and a high silk hat, and then the man ducked back. "Do you know a man called Frayne?"

Charlotte was gazing into a window, fiddling with her hair. She repeated the name a couple of times. "Can't say as I do, no. Why?"

"He followed us here from Madame Chou's." Zach took her arm and they walked past the restaurant and turned into another of the city's endless narrow side streets with sidewalks barely wide enough for two people to walk abreast. "Don't look back," he cautioned when she started to twist. "We don't want him to know we are onto him."

"Maybe Ricard sent him," Charlotte said, her voice tinged with fear.

"You mentioned him before. Who is he?" Zach felt her stiffen. She did not answer right away, and when she did, she sounded angry he had asked.

"I thought you would have figured it out. He's my pimp." Charlotte looked at him. "You never visited an opium den before last night. You've never heard of pimps. But I guess given where you're from, that's understandable."

"A pimp hires women to have sex with other men?"

"Hires them isn't exactly the right word. Forces them, is more like it. I was doing fine on my own, but I was in Ricard's territory and he sent his bullies to fetch me so he could explain how things are. They broke one of my fingers and would have done worse, but I agreed to go to work for him, so he set me up in that apartment building with a bunch of his other girls. I've been there four months, hating every minute. I wanted out in the worst way. Then you came along."

Zach thought she was giving him too much credit. "If you didn't want to work for this Ricard, why didn't you go to the police?"

The suggestion spurred a loud snort. "And have them laugh in my face? Do you honestly think they give a damn? To them I'm nothing but a whore. Besides, half the police force is on the take. They wouldn't haul Ricard into court. They would haul me in. Or throw me back to him to be beaten to death and dumped in the river. I'd rather go on breathing, thanks."

"That's not right."

"Welcome to my world," Charlotte said bitterly. "Nothing about this life is right, if you ask me. I once had a Bible pusher try to sell me on the notion of God and divine love and all that stuff. But what sort of God would let a girl go through what I've gone through? Where was all that divine love when my little finger was being snapped in half?"

Zach did not have the answer, and said so.

Charlotte shrugged. "No one does, I guess. Maybe there is no answer. Anyway, I'm used to it by now. I've learned that everyone is out to use me or hurt me in one way or another."

"Everyone?" Zach asked.

Giggling, Charlotte squeezed him. "Present company excepted. You're more of a gentleman than most of the gentlemen I've met." She sobered. "Now what are we going to do about Frayne?"

"Ask him why he's so interested in us." At the next corner, Zach turned right. They were in a residential district. Many of the homes lining the street had recessed doorways. He chose one at random and pulled her in next to him.

"Cozy," Charlotte said, and winked.

"Hush," Zach said, but he grinned.

They did not have long to wait. Jack Frayne walked swiftly past their hiding place, his neck craned as he scanned the street ahead. He had one hand in a pocket of his vest. "Where the hell did they get to?" he asked aloud.

Motioning for Charlotte to stay where she was, Zach stepped into the open. "Looking for someone?"

Jack Frayne whirled and jerked his hand from his vest pocket. In it he held a derringer.

Chapter Fourteen

Evelyn slept much later than was her habit. In the mountains, she was always up at dawn to help her mother with chores and cooking. Today she did not wake up until ten, according to the brass clock on the teak table next to the canopy bed. Sunlight streamed in the window and voices drifted up from the grounds below. She was surprised Athena Borke had not roused her. Ordinarily, Borke rose punctually at seven and had breakfast at eight.

Evelyn was in no hurry to get up. Her legs were sore from all the running she had done, and she had a few scrapes and bruises that hurt. The image of the alligator was fresh in her mind, and how close she had come to never seeing her parents and her brother ever again.

Each day she missed them more. Curling on her side, Evelyn gazed glumly at the barred window. She wished she were in her own room in her parents' cabin in the far-off Rockies, safe and secure from the horrors of the outside world. The white world, in this case. The world she once thought was so wonderful.

Suddenly, the bedroom door opened and Athena Borke

walked in without knocking. With her were the twins. Evelyn closed her eyes to pretend she was still sleeping, but Athena came over and stood beside the bed and said, "How stupid do you think I am, child?"

Evelyn looked up. "I have nothing to say to you."

"But I have plenty to say to you." Athena went to a chair and sat. "That ridiculous stunt you pulled last night could have gotten you killed. Mateo and Carlos told me about the alligator."

"I'll try to escape again if I get the chance," Evelyn said defiantly.

"Then it behooves me not to give you that chance. Should anything happen to you, it would spoil my carefully laid plans for your brother. Of course, it would be a while before he found out, and he might come after me to avenge your death, which could work in my favor, but I would much rather keeps things simple." She gestured at Mateo, who was holding a long box, and he brought it over and set it on the bed, then moved back. "I have a present for you."

"What is it?" Evelyn asked with no real interest.

"The dress you will wear when you come downstairs at one o'clock for the auction Edmund has organized. I selected it myself. The latest fashion for girls your age. Pink and frilly, with a lot of bows. You will look positively adorable."

"I won't wear it."

Athena sighed in annoyance. "Willingly or unwillingly, you will. I'll send up a maid at noon to help you get ready. If you refuse to cooperate, I'll have the twins hold you down for her."

"How many people will be at this auction?"

"No more than twenty, I should think, if that. We're holding it in the dining room, by the way. The light is good in there, and the guests can sip wine and nibble on cheese while they admire you."

Evelyn sat up. "I wish you were dead."

"Yes, yes, we've been all through that. But I'm not, and my whims are your commands. So you will do as I say and be ready by one o'clock." Athena rose. "I'll have a tray of food brought up."

"I'm not hungry."

"Did I ask if you were? You will eat what I provide or I will have the twins force it down your throat." Athena smiled and departed, saying, "Mateo, you will stay with her until the auction."

"As you wish, mistress."

Evelyn's fury was like a living, writhing thing inside her. She yearned to get her hands on a weapon, any weapon. In her mind she flashed back to when she was eight, and the morning they discovered Zach's pony dead in the corral attached to the cabin, slain in the night by a mountain lion. The other horses had been too scared to act up, and the cat had eaten its fill and padded off into the brush shortly before daybreak. Her father was set to go after it, but Zach insisted on going alone.

"You're being pigheaded," Evelyn had teased him. "But that's what brothers do best."

"If it were your horse, you wouldn't say that." Zach never could hide his feelings well, and when he was mad, as he was at that moment, it showed in every muscle, every pore. "I am going to kill that cat if it's the last thing I do."

"I like my horse, sure, but I wouldn't be as upset as you are," Evelyn had said. "I would never want to kill anything that much."

But she was wrong. She did want to kill that much. The closer the hour grew to one, the more she could not stop thinking about it. One of the maids arrived, a petite brunette in her twenties in a black uniform the maid mentioned was patterned after the style in France.

Evelyn absorbed her chatter without really listening. She had eyes only for the mirror, and the pink monstrosity Athena Borke demanded she wear. As sheer as silk, it had lace at the throat and at the ends of the sleeves, and small black bows across the bosom. It must have cost a lot of money.

"Don't you look beautiful?" the maid commented as she was fussing with the stays. "I would give anything to own a dress like this."

"You can have it," Evelyn said.

The maid tittered and patted at a stray wisp of Evelyn's hair. "Miss Borke bought it just for you. You should be grateful, not sulking."

"I am not a cow." Once, in St. Louis, her father and Shakespeare McNair took her to a cattle auction. McNair was thinking of buying a cow so he would always have fresh milk, but after talking it over, they decided that even if the cow by some miracle lived to reach the Rockies, a grizzly or wolves or the winter cold would do it in.

"Kids have the silliest ideas." The maid stepped back to admire her. "Mercy me, if you aren't as cute as a button. Now, don't muss your hair or rumple the dress. They want you at your very best when they send for you."

Evelyn glared after her, and when the door closed, said to Mateo, "You should be ashamed of yourself. Don't you have a sister? Or maybe a daughter somewhere?"

"I have five sisters," Mateo divulged, "and I would slit the throat of anyone who so much as touched them."

By the brass clock it was five minutes to one when the Creole opened the door and stepped aside for her to precede him. Her head high, Evelyn marched down the hall to the landing. Mateo was behind her every step. Gruff laughter and voices brought her to a stop, and she did not move until Mateo jabbed her.

Eleven people in addition to Athena Borke and Edmund Palantine were seated at the long table. Eight were men. The presence of the women shocked Evelyn. She had taken it for granted they would all be men. That there were other women as unscrupulous as Athena was deeply disturbing.

Palantine was relating a story that had everyone laughing. His leonine head turned toward the hallway, and he beamed and rose. "Ladies and gentlemen, I give you the princess of the hour."

All eyes swung around. Mateo gave Evelyn a slight push. She crossed to Athena and claimed an empty chair beside her. She couldn't bear to lift her face to the wicked scrutiny of the guests.

"Why, she's breathtaking!" a man exclaimed.

"She would make a fine addition to my stable," said one of the women. "May I have a closer look?"

"You all will in a bit," Palantine graciously replied. "For now, finish your drinks while Miss Borke tells you all about her."

"My pleasure," Athena said. "Her name is Evelyn King. She is going on fourteen. She has lived her entire life in the Rocky Mountains. You can count the number of times she has set foot east of the Mississippi River on one hand."

"Remarkable," someone said.

"You will never find a girl more innocent," Athena waxed on. "Real innocence. Pure innocence. Not the sham acting of the street urchins we deal with, who learn the facts of life before they're weaned. Nor the pretend innocence of those country girls who come to the big city for a new, exciting life. But the honest-to-God never-has-done-it-once-in-her-life innocence that is so rare in our profession." Athena touched Evelyn's hair, and Evelyn pulled her head away. "Think of it. Think of what that means. Think of how exquisite despoiling her would be." She paused. "With that in mind, Jasmine's comment about her stable requires that I clarify what should already have been made clear. This is a unique auction. You are not bidding for the right to put her in a bawdy house and see how much you can make off her before she turns bitter and hard, as they invariably do. No, you are bidding for the one-time-only right to do with her as you personally please."

A handsome man in an impeccable suit frowned. "No mention of this was made beforehand."

"There's more," Athena said. "You are to do it in front of her brother."

Surprise and incredulity spread from face to face. The cream of the city's underbelly glanced at one another, and at Palantine and Athena, and the woman called Jasmine arched a delicate eyebrow and said, "What is this? I can't decide whether to laugh or walk out."

"It is vengeance, my dear," Athena answered. "Specifically, part of my vengeance on this girl's brother for his part in the murders of my brothers."

"So you want him to watch—?" a man began, and threw back his head and cackled with mirth. "Why, that's diabolical. But I don't know as it's something I care to take part in. I like my lovemaking to be conducted in private."

"You always were a bit of prude, Vanker," Athena said, but she smiled to lessen the sting. "For those of you who share his high morals, make up your minds now whether you will bid or not."

Evelyn was aware of being the center of attention. She wanted to shrivel down into her chair. Or, better yet, to shrivel away to nothing. She could not believe that people would do this, that they could be so wicked and despicable. But if she had learned anything from her forced stay with Athena Borke, it was that there was no limit to the vicious depths to which human beings would go.

She had thought she was past being shocked, but she

wasn't. Maybe because it wasn't just Athena. Other people were involved. People every bit as vile. People every bit as evil.

Evelyn had learned more about the white world in the short time since she was taken captive than she had in all the years of her life. It was not the perfect world she imagined. Far from it. In certain respects, it was far worse than the world of her mother's people could ever hope to be.

The thought stunned her. For years Evelyn had tended to look down her nose at the Shoshones and other tribes. She always considered them backward compared to her father's kind. But the Shoshones would never do anything like this. Ever. It was unthinkable.

Everything had been turned topsy-turvy. Once, mere weeks ago, her goal in life had been to leave the Rockies and live in the white world the rest of her days. But could she still do that, knowing what she now knew? Maybe she needed to take a new look at herself and her dream. Provided she lived to have a future.

The fury that had been simmering deep within Evelyn boiled to the surface anew. She told herself that there was only so much a person could take. Instead of waiting for Athena's ax to fall, she should do what she could, while she could. There was only one way to end her nightmare. Only one thing to do. She had avoided thinking about it because it was not in her nature. But now she could no longer deny what had been staring her in the face all along: *She must kill Athena.* The decision came as naturally as breathing. It did not shock her. It did not fill her with dread. It was something that had to be done. She must stay alert for the chance, so when it came, she would be ready.

It was funny. Evelyn had never thought of herself as being anything like her brother. Or, for that matter, her father and her Shoshone kin. All of whom would kill when the need arose and not shed tears afterward. She had always thought she was above that sort of thing. That killing was what one did when one could not think of a better way. Oh, sure, there were exceptions. When an enemy war party attacked a Shoshone village, the Shoshones had the right to defend themselves. The same with her father and her brother when their lives were in danger. But this was different. Or was it? *Her* life was in danger, and had been from the moment Athena grabbed her. But until now, until this very moment, she had not taken the danger as seriously as she should. She had sulked and moped but not taken the one step she needed to take. She had bided her time, expecting her brother or her father to do what she should have done. She had ignored the truth. Well, no more, she reflected.

Athena was answering questions. "Yes, anything your heart desires. I don't care, so long as she is alive and more or less unharmed after you are done."

"More or less?" someone said, and snickered.

Jasmine leaned across the table and wagged a red fingernail at Evelyn. "How do you feel about all this, girl?"

"How do you think I feel?" Evelyn said sadly, only to see some of them smile and wink at one another. Her hatred grew to include everyone in the room. Sitting up, she folded her hands in front of her. "One thing you should know, if you are thinking of bidding." She looked at each of them, looked into their eyes, and she was proud that she did not flinch or show weakness. "I will kill anyone who touches me."

Athena raised a fist to cuff her, but the rest laughed in great amusement, and after a few moments she lowered her arm and snapped, "Watch that mouth of yours."

"Or what?" Evelyn taunted. "You'll have Mateo or Carlos slit my throat?"

"And deny myself the priv—?" Athena checked herself and said more evenly, "Not that it will ever come to that."

Any lingering doubts Evelyn had faded. Now that she had made up her mind, once and for good, a strange sort of calm came over her. A peace of mind she had not felt since leaving home.

Palantine had risen and was motioning for quiet. "My good friends, now that the preliminaries are over with, it's time to start the bidding. Take another look at the merchandise and ask yourselves whether you really want to pass her up."

"She is extraordinary," Jasmine remarked.

"The bidding will start at five thousand dollars."

Chapter Fifteen

Zach King had his Hawken leveled, but he did not have the hammer thumbed back. He had been careless. He went to cock it, but Jack Frayne thrust the derringer at his face and he saw that Frayne had not made the same mistake.

"Try it and you're dead."

Zach was tempted. All it would take was a flick of his thumb and a squeeze of his finger. But all Frayne needed to do was squeeze. Reluctantly, he eased his right hand off the Hawken and Frayne snatched it from his grasp.

Charlotte came out of the doorway. Instantly, Jack Frayne sprang back so he could cover them both and snarled, "Stay right where you are, tramp. This doesn't have anything to do with you."

"You're not here to fetch me back to Ricard?" Charlotte asked.

"I don't work for that two-bit pimp. I work for his boss. And my boss wants him." Jack Frayne dipped his chin at Zach. "The word has gone out, and I'm one of the messengers. Who would have thought I would be this lucky?"

Charlotte was confused, and it showed. "What are you babbling about?"

"Half the city is looking for this half-breed," Frayne related. "My orders were to spread his description among the less respectable element in this district and tell everyone to be on the lookout for him." Frayne chortled. "Now the money is all mine."

"I still don't understand," Charlotte said. "What money?"

"Never you mind." Frayne focused on Zach. "I want you to hand over your pistols and your knife. But nice and slow, if you please, one at a time. He wants you alive, but I'm sure he will understand if I have to put a bullet into your arm or leg to keep you in line."

"He?" Zach stalled. He gazed up the street. No one was near enough to notice that Frayne had a gun on him, and even if they did, not many would be brave enough to intervene.

"Edmund Palantine," Frayne said.

Charlotte had a strand of hair in her mouth and was gnawing on it. "I've heard of him. He's one of the richest men in New Orleans. He's Ricard's boss?"

"Hell, girl, Mr. Palantine controls every racket in this damn city," Frayne stated. "All the more reason for you to run along and mind your own business. You don't want to cross a man like him."

"What does he plan to do to Zach?"

"How would I know? I just work for him." Frayne sidled closer to the building. "Now, run along before I change my mind and take you along. Mr. Palantine might want to know what you're doing with this 'breed."

"I just met him!" Charlotte squealed. "He paid me to get up my dress and we were going to my place." She bestowed a fleeting sorrowful glance on Zach, then started back the way they had come.

Frayne barked at her to stop. "Just met him? Is that your story? May Ling told me the two of you spent all night at Madame Chou's." Frayne's brow knit, and he gestured. "I've changed my mind. I'm taking you with us. Don't look at me like that, girl. You shouldn't have lied." He faced Zach. "Now, then. You were about to hand over your weapons."

Zach could tell the man was nervous, and a nervous man was always more prone to be too quick on the trigger. He relinquished both pistols and his Bowie, which Frayne tucked under his own belt.

"Head for Canal Street. We'll take a carriage from there. Walk in front of me, side by side. No whispering. No touching."

Since Zach was not quite sure which direction to take, he waited for Charlotte to take a couple of strides and fell into step beside her. Out of the corner of his eye he could see her looking at him out of the corner of her eye. Her features shifted, and when he did not respond, her lips compressed and she made the same face, as if she were trying to get something across to him by her expression alone. But he could not see all of her face and he could not begin to guess what she was up to. He hoped she had the good sense not to try anything and get them both shot.

"Yes, sir, my lucky day," Frayne declared. He was in exceptionally fine spirits now that he had the upper hand. "A thousand dollars walks right into my lap."

"That doesn't make sense," Charlotte said.

"I thought I told you to keep quiet," Frayne warned, then: "What is so hard to understand, you stupid tart? That's how much Mr. Palantine is paying for your boyfriend, here."

Charlotte hissed through her teeth. "He's not my boyfriend. I told you, I hardly know him."

"And I told you to shut up." Frayne jabbed the Hawken

into her spine. "Or would you rather I blow a hole in you with this cannon of his."

Amazingly, Charlotte replied, "Kill a woman in broad daylight on a street crawling with people? How smart would that be? Go ahead and shoot. I just wish I could be there for the hanging."

"You're a fine one to talk about smart," Frayne said, and jabbed her again, only a lot harder, so hard she stumbled and nearly fell. "Mr. Palantine has some of the best lawyers in the city. And killing a woman is justified when it's done in self-defense."

"No one would believe I tried to kill you."

"They would when the police find my derringer in your hand. Now, for the last time, keep that trap of yours shut, or so help me I'll make it so you can't talk."

Charlotte finally heeded, and they covered block after block in silence. The pedestrians they passed hardly gave them a second glance.

Zach was racking his brain to make some sense of it all. He had never heard of an Edmund Palantine and could not imagine what someone so rich and powerful wanted with him. *Rich and powerful.* He knew only one person in New Orleans who fit that description. "Can I ask a question?"

"When you ask that politely, sure." Frayne added maliciously, "What's on your mind, 'breed?"

"Does the name Borke ring a bell? Athena Borke?"

"Can't say as it does, no."

Zach wondered if Frayne was lying. The man had hesitated before answering. If that was the case, and Frayne knew Borke personally or had heard of her, it meant Palantine must know her, too. Suddenly, it all made sense. Edmund Palantine was scouring the city on her behalf. A thousand dollars had been offered to whoever found him, money Frayne intended to collect. "Where does this Palantine live?"

"You'll find out soon enough. I said you could ask one question, not two. Button your lip and keep walking."

Charlotte's head moved slightly and she made the same expression she had earlier. Zach gave a slight shrug, and she frowned. Several women in bright dresses and wide hats were coming toward them, and she moved to one side to make room for them on the narrow sidewalk.

"Stop where you are," Frayne commanded, "both of you." He smiled at the women and bowed without taking his eyes off Zach and Charlotte, the derringer close to his leg so the women would not notice, the Hawken casually pointed at their backs. "Good morning, ladies."

A carriage was rattling toward them. Without warning, Charlotte darted behind the women and into the street, timing her sprint so the carriage came between her and Jack Frayne.

Frayne started to turn, but the women were smiling graciously at him, and he held his bow a few moments longer. By then the carriage had gone by and Charlotte was nowhere to be seen. "Where did the little whore get to?" He took a step and swore. "Damned tramp. She hasn't seen the last of me. What was her name?"

"She never told me," Zach lied. He was glad she was safely out of there. Now he could concentrate on Frayne without any distractions. He resumed walking when he was instructed to.

They traveled four more blocks. The street became congested with conveyances, the sidewalks filled to overflowing. Jack Frayne walked close behind Zach and pressed the derringer against Zach's lower back. "In case you get any notions."

Zach did not try anything. Sooner or later his chance would come. He could afford to be patient. Frayne had mentioned taking a carriage, so wherever Palantine lived must be some distance away.

The mouth of an alley loomed on Zach's left. Beyond it was an intersection, and crossing the intersection toward him were a pair of policemen. They had not noticed him yet. The street was too crowded. But in another minute they would. "Trouble ahead, Frayne."

"Where?" The black man craned his neck.

"Palantine isn't the only one looking for me. I was in a fight on a boat down at the docks. The police are after me, too."

"Sure they are," Frayne scoffed; then he stopped and gripped Zach's shirt. "Wait a minute. Was it the *Astoria*? The story was in the late edition of the newspaper yesterday, but it didn't mention you by name." He swore and steered Zach toward the alley. "Duck in here. With any luck, they won't spot us."

Buildings rose over two stories on either side, blocking out the sun. Refuse littered the ground, and the stink was awful. Frayne shoved Zach against a wall and pressed the derringer to his temple. "Not a peep, you hear me, 'breed?"

Zach sagged to give the impression he was thoroughly cowed. "Whatever you say."

Frayne stared anxiously at the street. The two policemen walked past without so much as a glance in their direction. Frayne exhaled and stepped back, lowering the derringer as he did. "That was close."

With the speed of a striking rattler, Zach struck. He grabbed Frayne's right wrist and twisted to try and make him drop the derringer even as he slammed Frayne against the opposite wall. Frayne started to raise the Hawken, but Zach smashed it from his grasp with a blow to Frayne's elbow.

Snarling, Frayne clamped a hand on Zach's throat. Locked together, they grappled fiercely, Frayne striving to bend his hand so he could shoot and Zach striving to disarm him. They struggled in silence. Neither wanted the police to hear them.

Zach spun, seeking to trip Frayne, but the man was bigger and outweighed him by fifty or sixty pounds and would not be budged. Suddenly, Frayne snapped his forehead at Zach's face. Zach jerked his head aside, and Frayne drove a knee at his groin. The knee missed, but not by much, and pain flared down Zach's leg clear to his toes. He tottered, off balance, and with a savage sweep of his shoulders, Frayne flung him bodily to the ground and dropped onto his chest, knees first.

Zach still had hold of Frayne's wrist, but now Frayne had the advantage and all it took was a powerful tug and Frayne's hand was free. Zach grabbed for it in vain, and stared up into the derringer's twin barrels of death.

Frayne did not fire, though. He opened his mouth to say something, but before he could, a firebrand in a cotton dress with a flower in her hair launched herself onto his broad back and raked his eyes with her fingernails.

"Don't you hurt him!"

With a howl of agony, Jack Frayne came up off his knees. Reaching back, he seized her by the hair and flipped her over his shoulder. She hit hard but sprang to her feet. Zach was upright, too. He lunged as Frayne turned toward him, blinking blood from both eyes, and again succeeded in clamping his hand around Frayne's wrist.

Frayne's other hand dropped to the weapons at his waist. Zach grabbed for that wrist, too, and they spun back and forth, Frayne growling like a beast and pulling and tugging, and Zach hanging tenaciously on.

In strength they were evenly matched. Jack Frayne was bigger, but Zach's life in the wilds had lent him sculpted sinews of solid iron. They skipped one way and then the other, neither able to best the other.

133

Then the firebrand in the cotton dress hurled herself at Frayne's legs, tackling him below the knees. Ordinarily, she would not be able to bring him down, but Frayne's momentum helped. He was moving so fast he could not stop, and her arms, ensnaring his ankles like vines, accomplished what Zach had not been able to.

Frayne cursed luridly as he fell on his side. The derringer and one of Zach's pistols went skidding across the dirt. Zach pounced, only to leap back as Frayne rose halfway and swung the Bowie as if it were a broadsword.

"To hell with taking you alive! I'm going to gut you and hand you over to Palantine dead."

Balanced on the balls of his feet, Zach awaited Frayne's rush. He had been in knife fights before, but not against someone Frayne's size, wielding a knife that could cleave his skull like an overripe melon. Frayne feinted, and Zach retreated, or tried to. He had nowhere to go. His back was to a wall.

A savage gleam lit Jack Frayne's dark eyes. He flicked the Bowie to the right, then the left. But he was not trying to cut Zach open. Not yet. Frayne was toying with him. "Any last words before I bury this to the hilt?"

Zach pretended to dart right but went left instead, toward the street, where he would have room to move. But Frayne was a step ahead of him and forced him back with wide swings of his own gleaming blade. One of those swings nearly separated Zach's head from his shoulders. The tip pricked Zach's skin but did not draw blood.

"You're quicker than a cat!" Frayne complained, planting himself between Zach and the alley's mouth. "But I've got you now. You can't get past me."

Zach intended to try. He skipped right and feinted left and went right, and he was almost in the clear when a big hand closed on his shirt and he was brutally slammed against the wall. He cracked his head, hard, and the alley spun in a macabre dance. The same hand closed on his throat.

"I'm going to enjoy this, 'breed." Frayne liked to hear his own voice, that was for sure. Instead of stabbing, he gloated.

The alley stopped spinning and Zach saw his own Bowie poised for a fatal thrust. They had both forgotten a certain white banshee who threw herself at Jack Frayne and clawed at his neck like a wildcat gone berserk. Frayne had no choice but to deal with her, which he did by letting go of Zach and turning and spearing the Bowie's long gleaming blade into her chest.

Charlotte crumpled without a sound, without a cry or a moan or a whimper, and Frayne cast her from him as contemptuously as if he were swatting a fly.

Zach saw her fall in a heap, saw the derringer near her foot. He had it in his hand before Jack Frayne could reach him. The Bowie flashed at his jugular, but Zach sidestepped and shoved half the derringer between Frayne's parted lips. It took only one shot. Muffled by Frayne's mouth, it was no louder than a slap would be.

Darting to Charlotte, Zach gently raised her head to his lap and felt for a pulse.

There was none.

Chapter Sixteen

Everyone had heard of Edmund Palantine, or so it seemed to Zach. Rich, powerful Edmund Palantine, who lived on an estate five miles out of New Orleans on Lafayette Road, which wasn't really a road but a winding ribbon of ruts and hoofprints.

Zach had long ago discovered that in the white world, the rich and the powerful were in a class by themselves. They enjoyed special status, special privileges. Lesser folk, those with less money, tended to regard the rich with an awe bordering on reverence. Everywhere the rich went, they were waited on hand and foot. Everything they did was food for public comment. Newspapers reported their comings and goings and doings with religious devotion.

Quite a contrast from a girl, say, like Charlotte, whose last name Zach never learned. In the white world she was not worthy of special attention or special mention. The poor never were. They were the nobodies. The shunned ones. Looked down on as inferior for no other reason than that they lacked the one commodity whites valued more than any other: money.

Money was their god. Many of his father's people claimed to worship the carpenter and the cross he bore, but Zach had seen through their deceit. It was money they craved more than anything else. It was money they would do anything to acquire. Money they would lie and cheat and kill for. Money they hoarded and exchanged and placed on a pedestal as the goal of their existence.

Zach wanted no part of their hypocrisy or their world. Give him the mountains and the plains. Give him the wilderness, where a man was measured by what he did and not by how much money he had hoarded.

Not that Zach would refuse a little money if it came his way. The purse he found on Jack Frayne contained more than two hundred dollars in coin and currency. He also helped himself to a gold pocket watch and a folding knife with a silver handle decorated with mother-of-pearl. It had been well oiled and opened with a flick of the wrist. The blade was four inches long, honed to razor sharpness. He fell in love with it at the first flick. He also took a ruby ring Frayne wore; it fit his middle finger quite nicely.

The bodies had to be left in the alley, Frayne's and Charlotte's both. Zach dared not draw attention to himself by carrying Charlotte to an undertaker's for proper burial. After dragging Frayne's body in the dim recesses, he gently carried Charlotte back and tenderly placed her on her back with her arms folded across her chest. He touched a fingertip to her lips and said softly, "I'm sorry."

Incredibly, no one had noticed the fight. Or if they had, they wanted no part of it or of him. When Zach emerged into the street, no one challenged him or tried to stop him or shouted for the police.

The first person Zach asked about Edmund Palantine was an old man hawking newspapers on a street corner.

"Palantine? Sure I've heard of him. Who hasn't? Big businessman. They say he has more money than John Jacob Astor. Word is he might run for senator next election. Has himself a fancy estate, but I couldn't tell you exactly where."

Next was an elderly man in a tailored suit walking a small dog in a park. The man gave Zach a critical look but replied to his question with "Yes, indeed I have. He's mentioned in the newspaper quite frequently. The last time was his annual charity dance. A pillar of the community, that Mr. Palantine. No, I don't know where his estate is."

Zach chose older men on purpose. It had been his experience in St. Louis and elsewhere that they tended to know more about the area in which they lived than younger ones who either hadn't been there that long or didn't really care. They were also less likely to pry into why he was asking.

He approached several others: a tavern keeper, a doorman at a hotel, two biddies who looked fit to bolt when he walked up to them. None could tell him where the great man lived.

All the while, Zach was conscious of the fact that at any moment he might stumble on the police or on Palantine's people who were searching for him. He kept one eye behind him, and while he was sure he was not being followed, twice he saw policemen and ducked into the shadows until they were well gone.

Luck finally favored him on Canal Street. A line of carriages were drawn up at the curb, waiting to be hired out. Some of the drivers were chatting and smoking; others were in their high seats, reading or dozing.

One driver in particular, an older man wearing white gloves, was reading *The Last of the Mohicans* by James Fenimore Cooper. Zach stopped and looked at the book, and when the driver glanced down quizzically, he commented, "That's one of my father's favorites."

"I admire his taste in literature. Cooper is one of my favorites, too." The man smiled and regarded Zach's buckskins. "When I was young I had dreams of being a woodsman, but here I am, sniffing horse farts for a living."

Zach had to laugh.

"You must be new to the city, son. Don't see many like you these days. I envy you in more ways than you can know."

The man went back to his reading, and Zach cleared his throat. "Say, mister. You wouldn't be able to help me, would you? I'm looking for a relative of mine. She works for a man called Palantine and lives in the servants' quarters on his estate, but I don't know where it is." Zach had noticed that the rich never did anything they could hire servants to do.

"I do. I've taken people there many a time."

And that was how Zach came to learn of the mansion on Lafayette Road. On the way out of the city, he stopped at a store that catered to hunters and fishermen. Any other time, he would have spent hours admiring the many guns and knives they had for sale. But today he was interested in one item and one item only. He was not sure they would have one, though. Whites were not known to favor them. But the husky clerk nodded and said, "Bows? You bet. We have one of the best selections anywhere."

Zach did not have time to make one. He had to settle for store-bought. It suffered by comparison to the ash-and-sinew bows the Shoshones made, but it was sturdy and powerful enough to drive an arrow through an inch-thick board, as the salesman demonstrated. A quiver went with it, and Zach purchased fifteen arrows with hunting tips. He had the salesman wrap everything and was almost out of the store when he thought to buy a coil of thin rope as well.

Zach decided to walk the five miles. It was late afternoon. The sun was warm on his face and birds were singing in the trees, but he wasn't in a mood to appreciate nature. He was thinking of Edmund Palantine and hoping his hunch was right and Palantine was somehow involved with Athena Borke. If so, Palantine might know where to find her, and when Zach found her, he would find Evelyn.

The farther he went, the fewer homes there were. The last mile, he saw an occasional mansion set off from the road, but he did not meet up with a living soul. He was in no hurry. He could not penetrate the estate until dark.

As things worked out, the sun was perched on the rim of the world when he came to an ornate gate with the name PALANTINE above it in large bronze letters. A high stone wall blocked his view. He was about to walk over to the gate and peer inside when two men with shotguns came from behind the wall and studied him coldly. He smiled and nodded and kept on walking.

Half a mile more, and Zach glided into the woods on the other side. Hunkering, he cut the rope a suitable length and tied one end to the end of the Hawken's barrel and the other to the Hawken's stock, leaving enough slack to slip his head and shoulders through.

Next he unwrapped the bow. He strung it as he had been taught, then pulled the string back a few times without letting go, getting the feel. He belted the quiver to his right hip and slid the arrows one by one into it. Slinging the bow across his back at the same angle as the rifle, he moved to the edge of Lafayette Road and waited.

Twilight faded to night. Zach ran to the wall and leaped. His outstretched hands caught hold of the lip, and he pulled himself up and over and dropped lightly to the ground below. Woods stretched before him. Unslinging the bow, Zach nocked an arrow to the string. He would use it only as a last resort. He did not want to kill if he could help it. He might be wrong about Palantine. Athena

Borke might not be involved. But if he had to defend himself, he could do so quietly.

Lights glittered off through the trees. Zach glided nearer. The mansion had a marble portico and a grand archway. More than twenty carriages were parked along a gravel loop. The windows were all lit, and piano music and voices hinted that a social event was under way.

Zach circled toward the rear. He scanned the windows as he went, careful not to be spotted. Suddenly, his whole body went rigid and he tingled from head to toe, overcome by conflicting emotions so powerful, they buffeted him like tempest-spawned waves on a rocky shore.

Framed in a window on the second floor was a stooped figure. Her small hands gripped iron bars inset into the sill, and her bowed forehead was pressed to them in sorrow.

The deepest relief he ever felt rendered Zach mute and motionless. But only for half a minute. Then the fiercest rage he ever felt galvanized him into stepping back into the darkest shadow and crouching.

"Evelyn!" Zach whispered, and saw her turn forlornly from the window and disappear. He smothered an impulse to race inside to her rescue. This time he must be smart. This time he would not let anyone keep her from him.

Time to rethink his strategy, Zach reflected. The people at the estate had to know Evelyn was there, had to know she was being held prisoner. That made them parties to her abduction. It also made them enemies who were bound to try to stop him from rescuing her. So be it.

His senses primed, Zach retraced his steps to the woods in front of the mansion. From there he glided toward the bronze gate and the guards with the shotguns. They were not hard to locate. They were leaning against the wall next to the gate and talking in normal tones.

Zach slunk forward until he could have beaned them

with a rock. Sliding an arrow from the quiver, he clenched it between his teeth. Then he drew back the string and sighted down the arrow already nocked. Taking a breath and holding it to steady his aim, he let the first shaft fly. It struck one of the guards between the shoulder blades and the man stumbled and toppled.

The other guard straightened. He might not have seen the arrow in the dark, but he heard it hit, and taking a step, he said, "Bill? What's the matter?"

By then Zach had the second arrow notched. He went for the head, and he did not miss. After dragging the bodies into the brush, he unloaded both shotguns and tossed them into a thicket.

Zach started for the mansion. He was halfway there when the undergrowth crackled, and sinking onto a knee, he raised the bow. Another guard was patrolling the woods, and this one had a large hound on a leash. They had not seen him, but they were uncomfortably close. He let them come closer. So close that when he loosed a shaft, he could hear the hound panting.

At the *thunk* the dog pitched forward. Its handler made the same mistake as the guard at the gate, and bending down, he said, "Rufus? What has gotten into you, boy?"

The bowstring twanged. The guard clutched at the feathers jutting from his chest, faltered a step, and collapsed.

Moving quickly, Zach circled to the same side of the mansion as before. The barred window was empty. He continued to the rear. Various outbuildings dotted a spacious lawn. Beyond was a wall, and beyond that tilled fields, and to the northwest, pristine forest. He waited long enough to satisfy himself that no guards had been posted, and was halfway erect when a pair of darkling figures came out of inky shadow near a rear door.

So there were guards, and they posed a problem. They were in plain sight of many of the windows. Zach could not resort to the bow, and to get close enough to use the Bowie, he must cross open ground. He toyed with the idea of making noise to draw them to him, but that was too risky.

Setting the bow down, he unfastened the quiver and placed the quiver beside it. Then he eased onto his belly and snaked toward the inky patch near the door.

The pair were chattering like chipmunks, just like the two at the front gate. They did not suspect a thing. Whenever either shifted or glanced in his direction, Zach froze. There were a few harrowing moments when he thought for sure they would see him, but he reached the mansion undetected.

One of the guards was complaining because he was hungry. "I haven't had a bite to eat all day."

"Whose fault is that?" the other responded as if he was tired of hearing him gripe. "You knew you had to stand a shift tonight."

The hungry guard rubbed his gut. "I can't wait for it to be over. The cook says there will be enough beef left over for me to gorge myself."

"There usually is a lot of food left. Palantine tends to do things in style."

"Overdoes things, you mean," the hungry guard said, and glanced quickly at the windows and the door, afraid he had been overheard.

"What are the festivities for this time?" the other one asked.

"It has something to do with the Borke woman and that little girl they've got locked upstairs. One of the maids told me they held an auction and the girl went for twenty thousand dollars."

"Hell, that's more than I'd make in ten years," the hungry one groused. "What's so special about her?"

"Beats me. You'd have to ask Palantine."

They walked to the far corner and turned, their shotguns cradled in the crooks of their elbows.

As motionless as a mountain cat, Zach tensed every sinew. When they were near enough, he sprang. The hungry one would never be hungry again; the Bowie slit his throat from ear to ear. The other guard tried to bring his shotgun to bear, but Zach buried the Bowie in his ribs and clamped his other hand over the man's mouth. After dragging them over by a shed, he wiped the Bowie clean on the hungry one's jacket.

The door wasn't locked. A short hallway brought Zach to a wider one. Most of the noise and activity came from somewhere to his right. He went left. He expected to come on a servant or someone else at any moment.

Stairs appeared. Zach climbed them three at a stride. If he had his bearings right, the room he wanted was the third or fourth on the right. He opted for the fourth but paused. After all this time, after so many weeks and so much hardship, they were about to be reunited. An odd nervousness gripped him, even as he squared his shoulders and gripped the knob.

Chapter Seventeen

The door was locked. Which was to be expected, Zach admitted, as he stepped back and kicked. It shook on its hinges but did not open, so he kicked it again, and a third time. Pain seared his leg from his ankle to his knee.

Inside the bedroom, Evelyn had jumped up from the bed, startled. She had been trying without success to sleep, but was still in her dress, not the nightgown Athena had bought her. She looked around for a weapon, but there was none. They had seen to that.

Again the door shook to a jarring impact. Evelyn backed toward the window, her hand to her throat. "Who is it?" she cried, fearful it might be Edmund Palantine. She was afraid, very afraid, and that would not do. She was a King, by God. Daughter of Nate King, the Grizzly Killer. Daughter to Winona, a full-blooded Shoshone who could handle a gun or a knife as well as any man. She refused to be scared. She would meet whoever came through that door as a King should.

Yet another blow resounded. Evelyn did not understand why her captors were trying to break the door down when they had a key. It must be someone else. As weary and drained as she was, the obvious did not occur to her until an instant before part of the door shattered and splintered.

Zach had been incensed that a last barrier was keeping him from his sister. He almost shot the lock, but reloading would take time and he needed his guns for what would come after. Lowering his shoulder, he barreled into the door like a battering ram. The next he knew, he was stumbling into a bedroom, and there she was. The shock rooted him in place. He had seen her at the window, but to be face-to-face after so many weeks rendered him speechless. But only for a moment. Heady, intoxicating joy coursed through his veins, and he opened his arms wide and said softly, "Sis."

Evelyn thought it must be a dream. After so long, her brother had come to save her. She had hoped and hoped and hoped, but always in vain. Again and again Athena Borke had outwitted them, to the point where her hope turned to despair. "Zach?"

Evelyn flew at him and he embraced her, and she buried her face in his buckskin shirt and burst into burning tears of the purest happiness. Zach held her tight, his heart hammering, his tongue feeling strangely thick, his throat congested, and whispered as tenderly as anyone had ever whispered anything, "It's all right. I'm here. You're safe."

Evelyn tried to speak, but all she could voice were choking sobs. She thought of all the times she had teased him when they younger, all the times when she had been as mean as only a sister could be, and she sobbed all the harder. "Oh, Zach."

Zach placed a hand on the top of her head, realized it was the hand holding his Bowie, and replaced it with his other hand.

Their bittersweet reunion was short-lived. Shouts had

broken out on the first floor and feet were pounding up the stairs.

"We must go," Zach said.

"Yes," Evelyn breathed into his shirt.

Prying her loose, Zach stared into the eyes he knew as well as he knew his own. "Are you up to this, brat?"

Only he ever called her that. Only he could do it with such affection. Evelyn blinked back tears and grinned and declared, "I am up to it."

"They're not getting their hands on you again. I'm killing every son of a bitch who tries to stop us."

"We are," Evelyn said.

"What?"

"*We're* killing every son of a bitch who tries to stop us." Evelyn had never used that word before, and she giggled. "I'm a King, remember? I was taught to shoot the same as you."

"Good girl." Zach's eyes were misting. He had to do something before he broke down. Drawing a pistol, he handed it to her. "It's bigger than the one Pa had custommade for you, but I think you can handle it."

"I can," Evelyn promised. "Give me the other one, too."

"Shoot when I say so, or if you have to." Zach's ears were drumming with more than his heartbeat; people were rushing down the hall. Whirling, he was out the door and among them before they reached the bedroom. Some were servants, a few must be guests, several wore the distinct dark suits of guards. He did not care who they were. Men or women, it made no difference. They had held his sister against her will. They had known she was there and they had done nothing. They were all going to die.

Weaving a crimson arc with his Bowie, Zach slashed right and left, high and low. He stabbed, he thrust, he chopped. Faces and limbs and torsos were ripped and rent and dismembered. So savage, so brutal was his onslaught, they fell before him like grain to a scythe.

"Out of our way!" The Creole twins Zach had last seen at the *Astoria* were at the end of the hallway. "Out of our way, damn you!"

Some tried to obey, but they were pressed too closely together. It hampered a guard with a shotgun who could not get a clear shot. He was lifting it when Zach's Bowie pierced his heart.

Scooping up the shotgun, Zach cocked both barrels. The Creoles had battered their way through the press and were almost on top of him. He unleashed both barrels full into their faces.

Buckshot was like grapeshot. It mangled bodies indiscriminately. The twins were blown apart. Others were wounded. Those unscathed turned to flee, but the floor was so slippery with gushing puddles of blood that many slipped and could not rise fast enough to escape the Bowie.

One of those down on his knees was another guard. Half his face had been blown off, but he was still alive.

Bending, Zach helped himself to the man's shotgun. Another guard was about to fire. He was faster, and made a sieve of the man's chest. That was the last of them. He came to the landing and squatted near the banister. Above the moans and bawling of the hurt and dying came shouts from below.

Evelyn touched his arm. "I'm still with you," she said. His face frightened her. She had never seen him so grim, so intense. "Are you all right?"

Zach did not say anything. He shoved the Bowie into its beaded sheath and unslung his Hawken. "When we reach the bottom, stick close. I'll keep them off you."

"I can help," Evelyn said, but he was already up and bounding down the stairs faster than she possibly could. A heavy flintlock in either hand, she ran after him, and was horror-struck to find the parlor filled with people who had heard the shots and the screams and come to investigate. Some she recognized: Edmund Palantine, James the butler, Vanker and Jasmine, and a few who had taken part in the auction. Many of the others had arrived early that evening for a cotillion.

"Who are they?" someone shouted.

"They have guns!" another cried.

Zach was nearly to the bottom when an armed guard charged through a door opposite him. The Hawken boomed, spitting lead and smoke, and the guard slid face-down to a stop at Zach's very feet. Snatching up the shot-gun, Zach slid the cord he had tied to the Hawken over his arm, and spun.

Everyone froze, the emotions of the guests ranging from terror to bewilderment.

"Which of you is Palantine?" Zach demanded in a voice that rang hard and fierce. "Edmund Palantine!"

No one spoke up, but more than a few glanced at their host, who darted into the dining room.

Evelyn was worried about more guards showing up. There were a lot of them on the estate, and they would come on the run. She reached her brother's side and said, "Forget him! Let's leave while we can!"

Zach swung the shotgun from side to side in case any-one got ideas. He still wanted to kill every last one of the curs, but he had Evelyn to think of. Getting her out of there was more important than his thirst for vengeance. "All right. But stay close." He started to back out.

Nodding, Evelyn imitated him, and then they both stopped cold in their tracks and her breath caught in her throat.

Athena Borke was in the dining room doorway, her fea-tures a mask of hate and contempt. "Go on! Run!" she shouted, shaking a fist. "But this isn't over. I'll track you down and pay you back for my brothers if it's the last thing I do!"

A roaring sound filled Zach's ears. The parlor and all those in it shifted and swirled, and when the world steadied itself, everything seemed to be bloodred. "We have to finish it," he heard himself say.

"Another time," Evelyn said. She was afraid for him. She knew how reckless he could be. There were too many for them to tangle with, and she could hear guards yelling out on the lawn. "Please. Let's go while we can."

Zach wavered, undecided, torn between his sister's safety and wiping that smirk off Borke's face.

"What's the matter, half-breed?" the object of his fury mocked him. "I can't believe you came all this way only to run off with your tail tucked between your legs."

A howl more bestial than human erupted from Zach. The people in front of him scrambled madly to get out of his way as he threw himself at the woman who had caused his family so much grief. Evelyn called for him to stop, but he couldn't stop now if he wanted to. Too much had happened. Too much suffering, too much sadness inflicted on those he loved most. He could not bear the thought of Athena Borke surviving to inflict more. He had to end it, and he had to end it now.

Her heart jumping to her throat, Evelyn ran after him. She saw Athena dart from sight. Saw, too, the devilish grin that lit her face. "Zach, wait! It's a trick! They're ready for you!"

Zach was vaguely aware that his sister had shouted something, but he couldn't hear her for the roaring in his ears. He was almost to the doorway when he launched himself through it in a rolling dive. Someone was behind the door. A gun went off and a slug struck the wall where his chest would have been had he been standing. He heaved onto a knee and twisted as Edmund Palantine loomed before him, a smoking pistol in Palantine's right hand, a pistol that had not been fired in Palantine's left.

"Die, you stinking 'breed!"

Zach fired first, loosing one barrel of the British-made shotgun into Palantine's belly. The blast not only smashed Palantine back against the wall, it blew his insides all to hell, leaving a hole the size of a melon.

"No!" Palantine bleated, and dropping his pistols, he clutched at his ruptured intestines and the other organs spilling from the cavity. "This can't be happening!" They were his last words.

Zach swung around. Nine or ten other people were in the dining room, most too stunned to move. He did not see Athena and wondered if she had made it through a door at the other end. Then a heavy blow jolted the back of his head and he sprawled forward, his whole body going numb. But he could turn his head, and there she was—the woman he yearned to strangle with his bare hands. She had been against the other wall. In her hand was a long brass candleholder she had taken from a nearby table. There was blood on it. His blood.

"This isn't how I wanted it to be," Athena Borke said as she stooped and picked up Palantine's unfired pistol. "I wanted you to grovel. I wanted to hear you beg for your life."

"Never!" Zach found his voice. The numbness was fading, but not rapidly enough.

"Never is a long time, boy," Athena said. "And time is one thing you're out of." She pointed the pistol and thumbed back the hammer using both thumbs. "Maybe it's just as well. You might have been run over by a carriage or hit by lightning or something before I got around to disposing of you, and I wouldn't want to deprive myself of the pleasure."

Zach sensed she was about to shoot, and he fumed at

the injustice of it all. Then a small, soft voice from the doorway seemed to fill the dining room.

"Athena," Evelyn said. She pointed both flintlocks. They were already cocked and her fingers were on the triggers.

Athena Borke glanced sharply around, then slowly shifted, her own pistol still trained on Zach. "Well, well. The child bares her claws. Put those down before you hurt yourself."

Silence had descended, both in the parlor and the dining room. Everyone was riveted to the girl in the pretty dress and the woman in black.

"I want to thank you," Evelyn said.

"Thank me?" Athena repeated, clearly puzzled. "Why in the world would you want to do that?"

"You have taught me that I am not who I thought I was."

"What the hell are you talking about? Are you stalling in the hope your brother will shoot me before I shoot him?"

"My brother is to stay out of this. You hear me, Stalking Coyote?"

"Yes," Zach answered. "I hear you, Blue Flower." He made it to his knees and leveled the shotgun at the others.

"Blue Flower?" Athena sneered.

"My Shoshone name," Evelyn said. "I have a white name and an Indian name, but I have never used the Indian name much."

"Who cares? Drop those guns or your brother is the next to die." Athena aimed her pistol.

"I won't let you harm him."

"Oh really?" Athena took a quick step just as a guard burst inside and snapped off a hasty shot at Zach; her step took her into the path of the bullet. The impact staggered her. She gaped in disbelief at the hole below her bosom and exclaimed, "No! Not like this! I won't let it be like this!" Pain hit her and she doubled over. Shrieking like a bobcat, she tottered a few steps, then raised her head and snarled, "I should have killed you long ago, you stinking little half-breed!" She raised her pistol, but her hand was shaking so badly, she couldn't hold it steady.

"Yes, I am half-and-half," Evelyn said. "I've tried to pretend I wasn't. I thought my father's people were better than my mother's people. I thought your world was the world in which I wanted to live. But I see now I was wrong. Both worlds have their good and their bad." She paused. "You are part of the bad."

"Who are you to judge me?" Athena spat. "You're nothing but a squaw's droppings." She sought to straighten but couldn't. A sheen of sweat caked her as she pressed her other hand to the bullet hole and hissed, "You're not fit to lick my shoes! Die, damn you!" But as she struggled to hold the pistol level, her legs buckled. She was dead before she sprawled onto the floor.

Chapter Eighteen

Evelyn did not feel a thing. Not any emotion at all. She stared at the blood oozing from Athena Borke and she did not feel happy or regretful or sad. "How peculiar," she said to herself, then started when a hand gripped her shoulder.

"We have to light a shuck, sis," Zach said. He was covering the guard, who had thrown his hands in the air.

A beefy man with large sideburns hooked his thick fingers into claws and lumbered toward them. "Filthy murderers! You're not going anywhere! Athena Borke and Edmund Palantine were friends of mine."

Another man stopped him, saying, "Have you lost your senses, Ricard? They'll do to you as they did to them."

Zach had begun to turn but stopped. "What did you say his name was?"

The beefy specimen with the sideburns answered for himself. "My name is Ricard, Emile Luc Ricard."

"This is for a girl named Charlotte," Zach said, and fired the shotgun into Ricard's face. Ricard's head exploded like a pumpkin, spraying hair and pieces of flesh and bone over everyone within a fifteen-foot radius. Stray buckshot struck a few of the others, but only Ricard's body fell near Athena's, his head gone except for a flap of sideburn and half of one ear.

A woman lost her supper.

"Sweet Jesus!" a man exclaimed.

From somewhere at the front of the mansion came harsh yells. More guards, Zach figured, and propelled Evelyn toward the rear wall. She was still staring at Athena Borke and did not seem to be aware of what was going on around her. "Snap out of it!" he said, shaking her. "We're not out of the woods yet!"

Evelyn tore her gaze from the woman who had held her captive for so long and roused herself with a toss of her head. "Sorry. I'm all right. What do you need me to do, big brother?"

They came to a window. Zach unfastened the latch and opened it as high as it would go, then literally shoved Evelyn through. In a heartbeat he was beside her in the night and taking her hand as they raced toward the stable.

"Thank you," Evelyn said.

Zach responded, "Save it for later, if we live." They still had a small army of guards to elude.

The stable doors were closed. Zach cast the shotgun aside and opened the right-hand door. Every stall contained a horse. Fine horses, the best money could breed. Bridles were in a tack room in the corner. He grabbed one for him and one for her. "We'll have to ride bareback." It would take too long to throw on blankets and saddles.

"So?" Evelyn said. Her parents had put her on a horse almost as soon as she learned to walk, and for years she rode her pony bareback. Opening the second stall, she slipped the bridle on a buttermilk. It stomped a hoof. Gripping its mane, she swung herself up and beamed. "Ready when you are."

Zach kneed his mount to the door. "Don't lose me in

the dark. If you take a bullet or your horse is hit, give a holler."

"You must think I'm awfully stupid," Evelyn teased.

"No, I think you're the best sister anyone ever had, and I care for you with all my heart."

Evelyn's ears burned and a lump formed in her throat. He rarely complimented her, and she could count on one hand the times he had expressed affection. Usually, all they ever did was bicker.

"Here we go," Zach said, and pushed the door wide open. Dark figures were at several of the rear windows and a rifle cracked as he reined around the corner and trotted toward the wall. Glancing over a shoulder, he ensured Evelyn was keeping up. She grinned at him. At that moment, he loved her more than he ever had.

"There's the back gate!"

Zach had already seen it. It was closed, but that was quickly rectified, and side by side they circled to Lafayette Road and headed toward New Orleans. For the first mile Zach held to a gallop, but after that he slowed to save their mounts for when their speed would be really needed.

Evelyn breathed deep of the night air and did something she had not done in more days than she could remember: She laughed. "I'm so happy, I could cry."

"Makes two of us," Zach said, "and Ma and Pa will show you all their teeth when we get back."

"I've missed them so much." Evelyn did not let herself dwell on it or she would break into tears. "What now? Do we go into the city or around it?"

Zach was mulling the same question. He would like to buy supplies and visit a gunsmith and maybe send a note to Alain de Fortier, thanking Alain for his help. But the police were still on the lookout for him, and thanks to Edmund Palantine, so was half of New Orleans. "I think it best we go around."

"And you know better than me."

"That's a first," Zach said, and they grinned.

Evelyn's elation lasted another mile. Then the drum of hoofbeats signaled they were being pursued.

"Took them long enough," Zach remarked, and guided her into the forest bordering the north side of the rutted road. They did not have long to wait before over a dozen guards and guests, armed and as grim as death, pounded past. Not until the riders were out of sight did Zach knee his mount from concealment.

"They're not very bright," Evelyn said. "They should have brought torches so they could track us."

"I doubt that bunch could track a herd of buffalo across a mudflat," Zach scoffed. When it came to woodlore, most whites, particularly city dwellers, were helpless babes. Not that all Indians were master trackers. Some were good, some weren't. It was the individual, not the lineage, that counted.

Half a mile from the outskirts of New Orleans, Zach again left the road and made off cross country. There were a lot of other towns and a few cities between Louisiana and the frontier where he could stop for provisions and visit a gun shop. In the meantime, they would live off the land.

"I don't mind," Evelyn said when he explained. Once, she would have. Once, she would have insisted on staying at a hotel so she could pamper herself with hot food she did not have to cook and a hot bath to relax her before she turned in.

"Sorry it took me so long to find you," Zach remarked.

"Don't be silly. I'm amazed you did it at all," Evelyn said. "I suppose we should be grateful to Athena Borke."

"Were you hit over the noggin when I wasn't looking?" Zach wasn't sure he had heard her correctly.

Evelyn snickered and shook her head. "No, I meant we should thank her for the favor she did you."

"I've lost your trail, little sister."

"Didn't you know? She never stopped bragging to me how she rigged your trial by bribing half the jurors so they would find you innocent of murdering her brothers. She thought the gallows were too good for you. She wanted to kill you herself."

Zach had to marvel at the woman's craftiness. "She should have been born a rattlesnake."

"I wish she had never been born at all," Evelyn said. She recalled the terrible auction, recalled its purpose, and shuddered.

"Forget her," Zach advised. "You're safe now, and you'll stay safe if I have anything to say about it."

Evelyn did not say anything. There was a time when she thought the world was a bright and shiny place as safe as a hug from her mother, when she took it for granted that nothing really bad would happen to her. Now she had learned better. Now she knew what her father had been trying to help her understand all the years she was growing up. He held the view that there were two kinds of people in the world, those who saw it as it was and those who saw it as they would like it to be. She had not realized he was talking about her. About the fluffy and nice pretend world she had made up. Because life was not all fluffy and nice. Life could be hard and life could be cruel.

She should have seen it sooner. But it was not wholly her fault. Her parents had sheltered her from hardship as much as they were able, and while there had been a few incidents where her life had been in peril, her day-to-day life was as peaceful and loving as anyone had a right to pray for.

Looking back through the mists of time, Evelyn saw their cabin as an oasis in a desert of burning hate, hot lead, and cold blades. The real world, the world her father tried to warn her about, would slit her throat or gut her and hang her out like a skinned raccoon if she did not always keep in mind that it could happen anywhere, at any time.

"What are you thinking about?" Zach asked. Normally she would be talking his head off.

"Growing up," Evelyn said.

"It's not much fun," Zach admitted.

Through the night they rode, and camped at daybreak in a glade near a creek. Zach cut whangs from his buckskins to fashion crude but serviceable hobbles for their mounts. Then they curled up under the spreading limbs of an oak. He tried to sleep, but he would wake up every hour or so with his heart hammering and then have trouble dozing off again. About one in the afternoon, he sat up for the fourth or fifth time. Careful not to awaken Evelyn, he slunk off into the brush.

They needed to eat to keep their strength up. Zach spotted a doe, but he did not shoot when it bounded off. A shot could be heard from a long way off, and posses were bound to be scouring the countryside. He was thinking he would try to bean a rabbit with a rock, which he had done before, but an obligingly plump gray squirrel came down out of a tree to chatter at him from a low limb, and he beaned that instead.

Returning to the oak, Zach gathered a handful of dry kindling, took his fire steel and flint from his possibles bag, and soon had a small fire crackling. The few tendrils of smoke it produced were dispersed by the boughs above. He butchered the squirrel and rigged a spit for the chunks of dripping meat.

Soon Evelyn stirred and opened her eyes and sniffed. "Something smells delicious." She rose on an elbow and licked her lips. "What did you get for you to eat?"

"Me?" Zach said, and chuckled. "Oh. I get it. Next time I'll club a cow and carry it back over my shoulders."

"Would you do that for me?" Evelyn sat up and leaned against the oak. "I can't believe we're really here. I keep thinking I'll wake up and find myself back in that bedroom."

"We're really here." Zach turned the spit to roast the meat evenly.

Evelyn had another worry she brought up. "Will they send the army after us like they did after you killed the Borke brothers?"

"I don't see why they would. This isn't a military matter." Zach tried to sound convincing, but secretly he suspected their bloodletting would haunt them later. Whites were more tolerant of whites killing whites than they were of half-breeds or Indians killing whites. "Don't fret your little head over it."

"My noodle is as big as yours," Evelyn bantered, tickled that they were as they had always been.

Zach speared a piece of squirrel with the tip of his Bowie and gave her the knife. "Try not to stab your tongue by mistake."

Evelyn ate ravenously. She was hungrier than she had been in weeks. Juice dribbled down her chin, and she swiped at it with a sleeve and chuckled.

"What now?"

"I'm me again."

Zach bit into his piece and happened to gaze at the horses. Both had their heads high and their ears pricked and were staring intently to the east. Jumping up, he stomped on the fire to smother the flames.

Evelyn did not ask why. She helped him, and did not complain when he practically threw her onto the buttermilk. As quietly as Comanches, they slipped away.

From the crest of a wooded rise a quarter of a mile

away they could see the glade, and the riders in it. "I count eleven," Zach said. The chase had begun in earnest.

For the rest of the day and on into the night, they put their mounts to a test of endurance. At midnight, Zach stopped. He persuaded Evelyn to sleep by promising he would soon turn in, but he did no such thing. He stayed up all night watching their back trail. Before dawn, he shook Evelyn and they were under way again.

By noon their animals were flagging and Zach's eyelids were leaden, but he permitted only a brief rest. He had not seen any sign of the posse, but that did not mean they weren't back there.

Along about two, they came to a swamp. Evelyn wanted to go around. Her encounter with the alligator was vivid in her mind and she would rather not encounter another.

"I think we should push on through," Zach disagreed. He realized the risk was great, but so was the potential benefit. He deemed it unlikely the posse would follow them in.

"Whatever you say, big brother."

"I could get used to this," Zach said.

For four hours they slogged through rank vegetation crawling with snakes and fetid pools swarming with insects. They were exhausted and dirty and bone sore when they came to dry ground, but Zach still did not stop. Again it was pushing midnight when he drew rein.

Evelyn was so exhausted, she was asleep the instant her cheek touched the ground. She did not wake up once during the night, and at daybreak she was refreshed and eager to head out.

Two more days passed. Two days where they did not come across another living soul. Two days where there was no hint of pursuit.

"We've given them the slip," Zach announced. "In a

David Thompson

couple of weeks we'll be in St. Louis, and from there it's on to the Rockies, and home."

"Home," Evelyn said. Back to the mountains she once despised. To the cabin in their valley high in the mountain, and a way of life she had been ready to forsake for the glitter and deceit of civilization. "I can hardly wait."

WILDERNESS

Mountain Nightmare

David Thompson

Frontiersmen are drawn to the wilderness of the Rockies by the quest for freedom, but in exchange for this precious liberty they must endure a life of constant danger. Nate King and his family have faced every vicious predator in the mountains, both human and animal, and triumphed. But what of a predator that is neither human nor animal…or a little of both? Nate and his neighbors have begun to find tracks and other signs of a being the Shoshones know as one of the Old Ones, a half-man, half-beast creature that preys on humans and kills simply for the sake of killing. Can the old legends really be true? And if they are, how can even the best hunter on the frontier survive becoming the hunted?

___4656-3 $3.99 US/$4.99 CAN

WILDERNESS

#28
The Quest
David Thompson

Life in the brutal wilderness of the Rockies is never easy. Danger can appear from any direction. Whether it's in the form of hostile Indians, fierce animals, or the unforgiving elements, death can surprise any unwary frontiersman. That's why Nate King and his family have mastered the fine art of survival—and learned to provide help to their friends whenever necessary. So when one of Nate's neighbors shows up at his cabin more dead than alive, frantic with worry because his wife and child had been taken by Indians, Nate doesn't hesitate for a second. He knows what he has to do—he'll find his friend's family and bring them back safely. Or die trying.

___4572-9 $3.99 US/$4.99 CAN

WILDERNESS DOUBLE EDITION

SAVE $$$!

Savage Rendezvous by David Thompson. In 1828, the Rocky Mountains are an immense, unsettled region through which few white men dare travel. Only courageous mountain men like Nathaniel King are willing to risk the unknown dangers for the freedom the wilderness offers. But while attending a rendezvous of trappers and fur traders, King's freedom is threatened when he is accused of murdering several men for their money. With the help of his friend Shakespeare McNair, Nate has to prove his innocence. For he has not cast off the fetters of society to spend the rest of his life behind bars.

And in the same action-packed volume...

Blood Fury by David Thompson. On a hunting trip, young Nathaniel King stumbles onto a disgraced Crow Indian. Attempting to regain his honor, Sitting Bear places himself and his family in great peril, for a war party of hostile Utes threatens to kill them all. When the savages wound Sitting Bear and kidnap his wife and daughter, Nathaniel has to rescue them or watch them perish. But despite his skill in tricking unfriendly Indians, King may have met an enemy he cannot outsmart.

__4208-8 $4.99 US/$5.99 CAN

Dorchester Publishing Co., Inc.
P.O. Box 6640
Wayne, PA 19087-8640

Please add $1.75 for shipping and handling for the first book and $.50 for each book thereafter. NY, NYC, and PA residents, please add appropriate sales tax. No cash, stamps, or C.O.D.s. All orders shipped within 6 weeks via postal service book rate. Canadian orders require $2.00 extra postage and must be paid in U.S. dollars through a U.S. banking facility.

Name_____
Address_____
City_____ State_____ Zip_____
I have enclosed $_____ in payment for the checked book(s).
Payment <u>must</u> accompany all orders. ☐ Please send a free catalog.

WILDERNESS
The epic struggle for survival
in America's untamed West.

#17: *Trapper's Blood*. In the wild Rockies, any man who
dares to challenge the brutal land has to act as judge, jury,
and executioner against his enemies. And when trappers start
turning up dead, their bodies horribly mutilated, Nate and
his friends vow to hunt down the merciless killers. Taking
the law into their own hands, they soon find that one hasty
decision can make them as guilty as the murderers they want
to stop.

___3566-9 $3.50 US/$4.50 CAN

#16: *Blood Truce*. Under constant threat of Indian attack,
a handful of white trappers and traders live short, violent
lives, painfully aware that their next breath could be their
last. So when a deadly dispute between rival Indian tribes
explodes into a bloody war, Nate has to make peace between
enemies—or he and his young family will be the first to lose
their scalps.

___3525-1 $3.50 US/$4.50 CAN

#15: *Winterkill*. Any greenhorn unlucky enough to get
stranded in a wilderness blizzard faces a brutal death. But
when Nate takes in a pair of strangers who have lost their
way in the snow, his kindness is repaid with vile treachery.
If King isn't careful, he and his young family will not live
to see another spring.

___3487-5 $3.50 US/$4.50 CAN

Dorchester Publishing Co., Inc.
P.O. Box 6640
Wayne, PA 19087-8640

Please add $1.75 for shipping and handling for the first book and
$.50 for each book thereafter. NY, NYC, and PA residents,
please add appropriate sales tax. No cash, stamps, or C.O.D.s. All
orders shipped within 6 weeks via postal service book rate.
Canadian orders require $2.00 extra postage and must be paid in
U.S. dollars through a U.S. banking facility.

Name_____
Address_____
City_____ State_____ Zip_____
I have enclosed $_____ in payment for the checked book(s).
Payment <u>must</u> accompany all orders. ❏ Please send a free catalog.

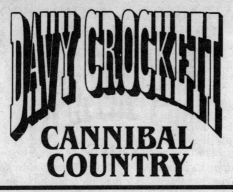

DAVY CROCKETT

CANNIBAL COUNTRY

David Thompson

Davy Crockett is driven by a powerful need to explore, to see what lies beyond the next hill. On a trip through the swamp country along the Gulf of Mexico, Davy and his old friend Flavius meet up for the first time with Jim Bowie, a man who will soon become a legend of the West—and who is destined to play an important part in Davy's dramatic life. Neither Davy nor Jim know the meaning of the word "surrender," and when they run afoul of a deadly tribe of cannibals, they know it will be a fight to the death.

___4443-9 $3.99 US/$4.99 CAN

GUNS OF VENGEANCE

LEWIS B. PATTEN

Incessant heat and drought have taken their toll on the Wild Horse Valley range. And nowhere is it worse than on the Double R, the largest ranch in the district, owned by Walt Rand. Things really heat up when Nick Kenyon diverts what little water is left in Wild Horse Creek, giving his little ranch more water than it needs and the Double R none. Kenyon had long since managed to turn all the smaller ranchers against the Double R, blaming Rand and his greed for all the problems on the range. But stealing water in a drought is the last straw, and Rand decides to fight back. He'll deal with Kenyon the same way he would with anyone who stole what belonged to the Double R—with bullets!